MARK'S CHOSEN

Creekside Township Rivals

Book 4

JT Fader

MARK'S CHOSEN Copyright © 2024 by JT Fader (Leigh Jarrett). All rights reserved. No part of this book may be used or reproduced in any manner whatsoever without written permission, except in the case of brief quotations embodied in critical articles and reviews. All trademarks are the property of the respective owners.

Published by Steambath Press
A Creekside Township Rivals Romance

Paperback published March 2024
ISBN-13: 978-1-998008-50-6

Chapter One | Mark

Today was going to be a good day. That's what I kept telling myself as I fiddled with the coffee pot. I needed a new one. This one spat and sputtered and took forever to put water through the filter. It annoyed me enough that I planned to venture into a store to replace it.

The drive into Riverton took more than a few minutes. My house was quite far out of town. The small sleepy township had a few shops on its picturesque main street. Not many, but there was a hardware store that sold small appliances. I had a few other things to pick up there as well.

I'd ordered some parts for the latest plumbing job I was working on. One of the humans in town was renovating their bathroom. A complete gut job. And the old plumbing was a mess.

After 30 years as a plumber, my work could be completed as easy as breathing. That's not what was getting under my skin. As leader of the Riverton pack, I had obligations. My Betas were on my case to find an Omega to settle and start a family with. I knew who my choices were. They were from my pack, the female wolves who were being presented to me as options.

Not a single one of them interested me. Even the ones I'd already rutted with. Not sure what my problem was. Maybe I was holding out for my fated mate to appear. They weren't anywhere in the vicinity. I'd checked here, East Creekside, and West Creekside.

Nothing. I'd felt nothing.

My heart wasn't sure I could simply choose someone and make a life with them.

I needed to figure my life out. At the age of fifty-three, I was long past the typical mating age. The Betas were right to fuss. The leader of their pack needed a potential heir.

I filled my to-go cup with coffee, a splash of milk, and three tablespoons of sugar. It was a bad habit—the sugar. I had a sweet tooth. I needed to run every morning to work it off.

This morning had been tough going. The snow was still fairly deep beneath the trees out of reach of the sun. And it was developing that icy crust that was uncomfortable on my paws.

After grabbing my keys, I set off down the steps to my truck. I'd recently redone the decal on the side. *Cooper's Plumbing – Because a royal flush beats a full house*. And a few playing cards in a royal flush fan along with my phone number. It was cheesy but I liked it.

I set off down my long driveway. The snow we'd had a week ago was compressed from all my trips up and down to the house. It was too cold for it to melt. More likely to become icy.

As soon as I thought that—my tires slipped. I'd need to pick up a box full of gravel and spread it on the driveway. I'd have a few other wolves help me. We all lived near my house.

Our pack was small. Only 12 of us. Aside from me, Hunter's sire, two Alphas, and their Omegas. One male Omega and three female Omegas. The three I had to choose from for a mate.

And the two Betas who were trying to force me to choose.

So far, our mated Omegas hadn't produced any pups. Unlike over in East Creekside where there was a pup explosion. Lucas and Adam were repopulating the valley all on their own. And Bryant's threesome had produced a second set of twins. I grunted and laughed. Jonas and his human mate had adopted a young human female so their daughter would have a sibling.

Their pack was thriving.

Ours was not.

I pulled onto the highway and turned on the radio. There were very few channels out this far in the wilderness. Riverton and Creekside Townships were towns that travelers drove through on their way to somewhere infinitely more interesting. We didn't even have accessible cell towers.

It suited me fine. I loved being so close to nature. I couldn't imagine living packed in a city with thousands of humans. Their scent in the air must be horrendous. The amount of crap they crammed into their bodies was stunning. Unlike wolves—who ate pure.

We hunted and gathered what the earth provided for us.

All three packs in the valley. The land was sacred to us.

I'd been spending a little time over in Creekside. Ever since we rescued Hunter and his unconventional family, I'd been bringing Hunter's sire over for visits with the pups.

It was nice to sit outside their little cabin in front of a bonfire as the pups played around our feet. I'd warmed more to Grayson than to Bryant. Grayson was quiet like me.

An observer. Very little escaped my eye. It made me a good leader.

Hunter was my much younger cousin. He was a handful to deal with. We'd never really meshed. A few years ago, he'd started annoying the humans. They'd come to me, asking me to rein in his flagrant displays of homosexuality. I'd chased them, teeth barred, out of my house.

Hunter's sexuality was his own to rejoice in. When he'd painted his house rainbow colors, though … that had been a step too far.

We'd argued. He'd refused to listen to me. I could have ordered him to obey but that's not how I ran my pack. Omegas had an equal voice to the Alphas.

After many months of visits, and with two more adorable additions to their family, Hunter and I were getting along well enough. I was proud of him. He'd fallen in love and didn't let stigma stand in his way. Now, their poly relationship was barely an item of conversation.

I made my way down Main Street and pulled into a parking stall outside the hardware store. The street looked almost deserted. Only a few cars. It was a wonder the stores stayed open.

Harkell's Hardware. I pulled open the door and wandered into a place that made me happy. The walls were lined with a wash of hooks holding different items. Small bins underneath at waist level and larger items leaned up against the wall beneath those. Down the center, more bins piled full of bits and pieces of every tool and gadget imaginable.

Toward the rear of the store were the small appliances. Beyond that, the commercial hardware items overflowed into a warehouse area around the back. I needed to visit both places. I perused the coffee pots first. They all looked the same. I picked the cheapest one. Probably not the most solid choice but I'd been putting up with my old one for years. Anything would be better.

I met the human owner Brett out back. He was fussing with organizing orders.

"Morning," I said.

"Mine got off to a rocky start," Brett replied. "Shipments are late. People are pissed."

"Tiles again?"

"Always. Doesn't matter how much room I leave; the tile companies always outdo themselves in their ability to miss a shipment date."

"Luckily, my job isn't tiling. Have you got the copper piping I ordered?"

"Yes." Brett strode off toward a heap of construction materials. Two-by-fours, sheetrock, insulation bundles. Beyond them, the copper I needed for today. "It's all there."

"Awesome." I lifted the lengths I needed. "Put them and this coffee maker on my account?"

"For sure. Enjoy the rest of your day." He waved at me and went back to his orders.

I'd known Brett since I was a kid when my sire first brought me into the store to buy supplies for his construction business. He was one of the few humans I was friendly with.

He was *long* past the age for retiring. He wouldn't hear of it, though.

Light flakes of snow floated out of the sky as I loaded the copper piping into the box of my truck. I set the coffee maker on the floor of the passenger seat.

I was rounding the front of my truck to climb in when a soft, aggravated, hissing voice caught my attention over my left shoulder.

"Fucking hell," it said.

I turned to find a young male Omega wolf struggling with an armful of bags. Poised on top of one of the paper bags was a carton of eggs that were about to find their way onto the ground.

I rushed over to help.

"Here, give me this bag." I scooped the unruly bag. It was heavy with items for a wolf's shopping trip in a human grocery store. The young wolf grunted and then sighed.

"I'm sorry. Thank you." He looked up at me. He had the purest pale blue eyes rimmed by incredibly dark thick lashes. They stunned me a little. I had trouble responding.

I cleared my throat. "Didn't want those eggs splattered all over the sidewalk."

"That would have been my weekend plans ruined."

"Glad I could save those plans for you."

The wolf nodded at me and jerked his head. "That your truck?"

I smiled. "I know. Cheesy."

"No, it's funny." He shifted his remaining bag into his other arm and unlocked the car parked beside me. With a key. It was an old car. Something that had survived from the 90s.

The way he placed the bag on his passenger seat seemed odd. He handled the bag strangely. He turned and I handed him the other bag. None of my business.

He slammed the passenger door. "Thanks again."

"Any time." I was curious about him. I hadn't seen him in town before. I would've remembered those eyes. "You're not from around here, are you?"

"Creekside." He walked back onto the sidewalk. "We don't have a health food store."

"So, you come all the way here?"

"Not usually. I have a special reason." He placed one hand on his stomach.

"You're expecting?"

"Another 2 weeks."

"Your first?"

He nodded and furrowed his brow.

"You and your Alpha must be excited. Are you from East Creekside?"

"Yes."

"Wow, your pack keeps growing in size."

The young wolf sighed. "Yeah." He gave me a half-smile but there was such sadness in those beautiful eyes. It was heartbreaking. "Gotta go. Thank you again."

He bustled past me, climbed into his car, and shut his door.

"Sure," I said to myself and went to my vehicle. As I sat in my truck, flipping through my notes for today's job, my concentration was broken by the sound of a car not quite starting.

Occasionally, it would start running and then it would sputter to a stop.

I wasn't surprised when the wolf appeared at my window. I rolled it down.

"Car trouble?" I asked.

"I know you're a plumber, but do you know anything about cars?"

"A little. Let me have a look." I spilled out and made my way to the front of his car. It made a clunk as he released the hood. I lifted the hood and braced it with the *hook thing*.

Okay, I knew very little about cars. I was hoping it was something obvious. Although, I'm not sure what I'd do if the problem jumped out at me. I sighed as I looked at the engine. It had seen better days. That much I could figure out with my limited knowledge. The car should be in a scrap heap. The young wolf stood beside me. He was almost as tall as me and he was bulky.

"Any ideas?" he asked.

"None."

"Is there somewhere I can call?"

"*Dieter's Motors* would be your guy. But he's out of town for a few days."

"Just my luck." He turned and sat on his bumper. "I'll have to call Lucas to come get me."

"Why not your Alpha?"

He wrapped his arms around his middle. "He can't."

Why?

His Omega was pregnant.

Again ... mind your own business.

"It'll take him an hour to get here," I said. "You could wait in the coffee shop."

"Nah, I'll sit in my car."

I grunted. I didn't like the idea of that. He would be too cold without a heater running. "Give me a second." I patted him on the shoulder and went back inside the hardware store.

"Brett, could I borrow your phone?"

He turned it toward me. "All yours."

I dialed the number of today's plumbing job.

"Carol, hey, it's Mark of Cooper's Plumbing. I've had something come up."

"Can it wait?"

"No. A buddy is stranded—car trouble."

"I need you here today. The tile is going in tomorrow."

"Actually, no. I'm at Harkell's. No tile orders are coming in today." I looked at Brett and he nodded at me, confirming what I'd said.

Carol sighed. "So many delays."

"That's construction for you."

"Okay. Hopefully, we'll see you tomorrow."

"I'll be there."

I ended the call and turned the phone back to Brett. "Thanks."

"Is he going to leave his junker car in front of my store?"

"Only until Dieter is back."

Brett shook his head. "It looks bad."

"It's just a car."

"Is he one of your kind?"

"A wolf? Yes. Why does that seem to be a problem?"

"Just never seen him before."

"He's from Creekside."

"And that doesn't bother you? Isn't he a rival?"

I looked out the window at the young wolf. He was dropping the hood back down. Again, awkwardly in his movements. Something was up with one of his arms.

"Might be, but he seems harmless enough."

In the past, our two packs, Riverton and East Creekside, would have been leerier of each other. All my trips out that way had brought our two packs closer together. I still had to ask for permission to approach their property ahead of time from Lucas. That wouldn't change.

The only other way onto the property was if I was with someone from the East Creekside pack. "See ya, Brett." I nodded and headed back outside.

"Okay," I said to the young wolf. "I'm going to give you a ride home."

His brow furrowed. "You don't have to do that." It seemed to come naturally to him, the furrow. His expression even resting was surly. I could tell he was the brooding type.

He was attractive, though. Now that I was looking at him straight on, I could see how broad his shoulders were. His winter coat covered a lot. He had one hand tucked away inside his sleeve.

"I don't mind. It'll give me a chance to visit with Hunter."

"You know Hunter?"

"He's my cousin. I visit him at least once a month."

"He's got his hands full. Not sure how they all fit in that small cabin."

"They seem to be managing. There are plans to build them a house."

"Yes, Lucas told me." He sighed. "Or they could have my house. I don't need all that space."

I laughed. "Knowing your pack, you'll fill that home in no time."

The wolf sniffed and extended his left hand. "I'm Reese Armstrong."

It made for an awkward shake. I was right-handed. "Mark … Cooper."

Reese released a small laugh. His expression lit up a little. "Like your truck says."

"That would be me." I jerked my thumb at my truck. "Should we go?"

"You really don't have to. My pack leader will come to get me."

"Like I said. I wouldn't mind a visit with Hunter."

Reese nodded and opened his passenger door where the groceries were located. "Can you help me with these? It's difficult for me to lift them from the car. I usually have someone help me."

"Of course." After I retrieved the first bag, Reese took it from me. Again … awkward, wrapping the arm where his hand was hidden in his sleeve around the bag.

We stored his two bags in my backseat on the floor. I remembered I had the coffee maker on the passenger side and relocated it in the backseat as well.

Reese climbed into the truck, using his left hand to hoist himself up. He struggled with the seatbelt but soon had it done. I brought the truck to life and cranked the heat.

The temperature outside was dropping and the snow was descending in thick flakes. I had to clear my windshield with the wipers before I pulled out of my spot onto the street.

I glanced over at Reese. His left hand was inside his right sleeve, massaging his right hand. I turned my attention back to the road. But after a few minutes, I snuck another glance.

The action must have been obvious.

"It aches sometimes," Reese said. "Especially in the cold." He pushed his right sleeve back. Instead of a hand, he had a stump covered in what looked to be a black sock.

"I didn't mean to—"

He caressed the stump with his left hand. "No, it's all right. I'm used to people staring." He pulled his sleeve back over it. "I'm still adapting."

"You weren't born that way?"

"No." Reese scowled. "Hunting trip. Found an old leghold trap the hard way."

"And you're still adapting? When did it happen?"

"It's only been three weeks. The trap was hidden beneath the snow."

I wasn't sure what to say. A wolf missing a paw would make life difficult. His Alpha should have accompanied him on this shopping trip. Driving must have been hard for him to do.

None of your goddamned business.

"I used to be a plumber like you," Reese said. "My brother and I have a company."

"You had to give it up?"

Reese looked out the window. "Couldn't manage to do the simplest things."

"Did you find other work? Or does your Alpha support you both?"

I know … none of my business. But I was curious about his Alpha. Reese seemed like a decent wolf. I hoped someone was helping and supporting him.

"I'm working toward becoming a published author."

Now that was interesting. It was rare to find a wolf working outside the trades in the valley.

"Have you written a book?"

"Still working on it."

"What's it about?"

"It's a dark detective mystery set in Seattle."

"Dark?"

"There's graphic murder and a brutal kidnapping."

I couldn't help but feel like that subject matter suited Reese. He gave off an angst vibe. I wouldn't be surprised if his mind was an anguished place.

We fell silent after that. I toyed with the radio but wasn't getting a clear signal from anywhere. Reese seemed content to stare out the passenger window, cradling his right arm.

I couldn't imagine what he'd gone through. He must be stressing about having a pup. Lifting and holding a squirmy bundle of fur was going to be a challenge.

Through the thick falling snow, I found the bottom of the East Creekside pack's driveway. It was touch and go making it to the houses at the top of the slope. My truck struggled even though it was 4-wheel drive. There was slick ice just beneath the coating of snow.

"Which is your house?"

"Third one down."

The East Creekside compound was all log homes except for one at the end of the driveway. Jonas' craftsman-style home stood out. Reese's house was small but looked inviting. It still had Christmas decorations up. A festive wreath on the door and lights along the eavestrough.

I pulled my truck up front and hopped out. I lifted both the bags into my arms and followed Reese to his door. I kicked the snow off my boots before entering.

"Sorry about the mess," Reese said as we entered the kitchen.

I was taken aback. There were dirty dishes everywhere. I looked for a dishwasher. There wasn't one. Everything had to be washed by hand. And his Alpha wasn't doing it. With Reese missing a hand, something as simple as washing dishes would be a monumental task.

I was becoming annoyed.

I set the bags down and started emptying them. It was the least I could do. Beneath two cartons of eggs was container after container of berries. All sorts.

"You like berries," I said.

"I read they were good for the pup. I wanted organic."

The second bag was full of meat. *Raised without antibiotics*. Reese was serious about providing the best for his pup. I opened the freezer. Inside were three bundles wrapped in butcher paper with the word *venison* written on the side in black grease pencil.

"Which meat do you want to leave out?" I asked.

"The two steaks, please."

I packed the remainder of the meat in the freezer and put the rest of the groceries in the fridge. Reese had popped open a container of strawberries. He was devouring them.

The young wolf had a good appetite. I watched him for a moment. He had a beauty about him despite his disheartened expression. If I had to guess, he was in his late 20s. Late for bearing his first pup. Maybe he'd waited and found his fated mate.

"What does your mate do for work?"

Reese didn't even look up. "Plumber."

"That must be nice. Having something in common."

Okay, I was digging. I wanted to know who this wolf was who would leave his pregnant Omega to fend for himself and not even help with the damned dishes.

Reese sighed and closed the berry container. He placed it with the others in the fridge. Apparently, I'd hit on a sensitive subject. I decided to withdraw.

"I should go."

There was that half-smile again. "Thanks. I appreciate the ride."

"It was a nice drive." I looked out through the kitchen window. The snow was coming down hard. "I might skip visiting Hunter. Looks like we're headed for a whiteout."

Reese glanced out the window. "Yeah, you should get going."

I found myself hesitating. I didn't like the idea of leaving Reese alone in that house. I might have a word with Lucas. His pack should be stepping up and helping this Omega.

I'd phone him once I was home.

Reese saw me to the door. He'd removed his coat. His long-sleeve, flannel shirt was tight against his swollen belly. I smiled. He looked like a pregnant lumberjack.

I jogged down to my truck and fired it up. I needed to turn around to head back down the driveway. There was space between two houses I could pull into. Once at right angles to the houses, I backed up, cranking the wheel. Reese shouted at me from the door, but it was too late.

My back tires slid down an embankment that was hidden by the snow.

There was no way I was getting out of there without help.

Chapter Two | Reese

I felt terrible. I should have warned him. The backend of Mark's truck had slid down the embankment at the edge of the driveway. And the snow was coming down in clumps.

I dashed down to his truck. He rolled down his window.

"I am *so* sorry. I should have told you about that slope."

"Don't be. I should have looked around before trying to get out."

"I'll get Lucas and Adam and a few of the other wolves."

"Appreciate it."

I ran to Lucas' first. I wrapped my arms around my chest. I hadn't put my coat back on. It was freezing. The wind was picking up, swirling the snow, limiting visibility.

I knocked on his door.

Adam pulled it open. As usual, there was a carousel of pups around his feet.

"Reese, what are you doing out without a coat?" He pulled me inside and closed the door.

"My car broke down."

"That doesn't explain why you don't have a coat."

"I was in Riverton. I got a ride home with the leader of the Riverton pack."

Adam crossed his arms. "Still not explaining much."

"He came in. Helped me put my groceries away. I took my coat off." I looked toward the door. "His truck is stuck. He backed down that embankment. I dashed out to talk to him."

"I'll get Lucas. Can you watch the pups while we see if we can help?"

"Sure. Thank you."

"I'll call a couple of other wolves to help." Adam strode off, furry pups following as he called out for Lucas, telling him his muscles were needed. Lucas answered with a sexually suggestive response. I blushed, the flesh of my ears heating. Our two leaders were incorrigible.

They both came back wearing winter coats, warm chunky boots, and gloves.

"We might have to tow him out of there," Lucas said to Adam.

Adam stopped beside me. "Try to keep Charles from chewing anything."

"Do my best. Thank you."

I was left in a house full of exuberant pups. Only three shifted to whom I could speak and knew they were listening because they would respond verbally. They weren't old enough to be part of the pack's link yet. That would happen when they were sixteen and shifted back for the first time. It was a cause for celebration for every pack and always followed by a hunt.

The unshifted furry masses followed me into the living room. I'd babysat for Lucas and Adam before when they needed a night out away from the chaos.

That was before I lost my hand. I approached the roaring fire to warm myself. I was glad of the wrought iron fire guard. I wouldn't have to be concerned about the pups singeing their fur.

The roaring of truck engines had me wandering over to a big window and looking out at the driveway. Lucas had his truck hooked up to the front of Mark's truck with a metal chain.

They were attempting to haul him out.

Unsuccessfully.

Now I felt *really* terrible. Mark had been nice enough to give me a ride home and now his truck was stuck in the middle of what was turning into a blizzard.

Some of the wolves from Carina's house were shoveling gravel under Mark's rear tires. It didn't help. The spinning of his wheels just spat it out.

I had a sinking feeling in my gut as it appeared they had given up. It would be the right thing to do to have Mark in my home until the weather cleared and we could call a tow truck.

I didn't like anyone in my house. I knew that's why it was such a mess. Lucas had offered to send wolves in to clean up and finish the many, many renovation jobs my mate had started.

I'd been too depressed to see anyone other than to have someone carry my bags into the house when I couldn't manage. They all had the same look on their face as Mark.

I wasn't coping well.

I knew I had to pull myself together for my pup, but the task seemed insurmountable. Most days and nights found me on the sofa, watching movies, and crying.

I couldn't stop crying.

A part of my brain still thought my mate would walk through the front door and I'd race to him to cover his face in kisses. I'd love him deeply. We'd been so in love.

My fated mate had been the absolute love of my life.

I fought the tears as Lucas, Adam, and Mike came inside.

"We'd appreciate the help, Mark, thank you."

I sniffed and pinched my nose. Adam offered me a gentle smile. He'd been amazing. The only wolf I'd let into my feelings. He'd held me as I'd cried many times. Listened to my endless stories about my mate. We had similar backgrounds. My fated mate had moved into town, a rival to our plumbing business. Lucas had allowed him to stay. We'd only lasted a week away from each other before we'd mated. It had been love at first sight. True enduring love.

I had been in heat. My mate had filled me with a pup.

I placed my hand on my stomach.

A week after we knew we were expecting, my world had come to a crashing end.

"You all right?" Adam asked.

"It's been a hard day."

"I'm here for you." He took my hand in his. "Always."

I nodded. "I know."

"Mark is going to help us shovel some of this snow as it falls to keep the driveway clear."

"Is the tractor still broken?"

"Waiting on a part."

"You staying in or do you want me to watch the pups?"

"I'm on hot cider duty. You can head home."

I watched the two Alpha males head back outdoors. A month ago, I would have been helping them shovel. Now, I was useless. I couldn't even keep up with my dirty dishes.

I said goodbye to Adam and walked back home. I closed the door behind me. It was so empty in there. All the life had been sucked out of it when I lost my mate.

Peter.

My Peter.

I sat on the sofa and cradled my belly. This would have been the first pup of many. We had admired Lucas and Adam. Filling our home with abundant love and joy had been our goal.

Tears rolled down my cheeks.

Ripped away from me—from us. I had nightmares of the night the sheriff showed up at my door at 7:56 in the evening. I'd been waiting for Peter to arrive home. Watching the clock.

My heart had been ripped out.

Gone.

He was gone.

I had felt my soul leave my body.

Now I was an empty shell. The only bright spot in my life was this pup. All I had left of Peter. A part of me wanted the pup to look like him. A part of me didn't. Would it be too painful to see his face staring back at me again? I wasn't sure.

My stomach growled. I needed lunch. My pup needed to be fed.

I removed one of the steaks from the fridge and forced myself to eat it. My appetite for meat wasn't improving. My morning sickness had been bad. Some smells still made me nauseous.

Raw meat was one of them. I tried cooking my meat to see if that would help but that was worse. I preferred my glass of raw eggs which I drank while I watched movies.

I finished my meat, covered myself with a blanket on my sofa, and laid down for a nap.

Nightmares plagued me as I slept.

There was a knock on my door that woke me from the hell I'd been sleeping in.

I was reluctant, but I opened it. It was Mark and he looked frozen. His clothes were encrusted with snow, and he was holding a metal lunch box in his gloved hand. His cheeks and nose were an angry, ruddy crimson. His beanie was like a white cap atop his head. Grey and brown wispy curls peeked out from the woolen edge; his hair beaded with drops of water from melted snow.

My stomach stirred a little. He was pleasant to look at.

Except he looked miserable.

"Oh, my god, come in." I stepped back to let him in.

"It's cold out there. We got two houses done, though."

"Best to stay ahead of it."

"Not sure we'll be able to keep up. The snow might go on all night."

"We usually use a tractor, but it's broken down."

"Bad timing."

"For sure." I reached for his lunch box. "Let me put that in the kitchen. We need to get you out of those clothes." I pointed down the hallway. "The laundry room is at the end."

I joined him after setting his lunch box on the kitchen table. He'd removed his coat, a sweater, and his socks. "Let's put everything in the dryer. Here …." I pulled a clean pair of sweatpants, socks, and a sweater from a laundry basket. "Put these on."

"Thanks. Wasn't enjoying the icicles in my pants."

"Don't blame you." I set the dryer and then left him alone to change. Hot cider sounded like a good idea. I found a clean pot, poured two cupful's into it, and set it on the stove.

Mark wandered into the kitchen. He smelled good. Like fresh clean air.

"Can you start a fire in the fireplace?" I asked him. "Everything should be there."

"On it."

I kept stirring until the cider was steaming. After I poured it into cups, I managed to grab both cup handles in one hand. I brought them to the living room. Mark had the fire started.

I set the cups on the coffee table. "I'll grab your lunch box."

Mark rose to his feet. "No. You sit. Enjoy the fire. I'll get it." He moved quietly to the kitchen. There was a confidence about him. More than just being a pack leader. At the same time, he was such a gentle and considerate wolf. I didn't mind him being here with me. I cozied up on the sofa under a blanket and sipped my hot cider. Mark sat beside me and opened his lunch.

I was assaulted by the scent of raw meat. I lifted the cup so the steam infused my scent receptors with the aroma of apple. He growled as he ate, my proximity setting him off.

I would have moved if I needed to but he stayed civilized.

So civilized that he even had a wet wipe in his lunch box to clean his hands.

Once finished, he collected his cup of cider and leaned back on the sofa. The golden light of the fire danced in his soft brown eyes. He took a sip. "This cider is good."

"Adam makes it. He gives us jugs of the stuff."

"Lucky."

I laughed. "By the end of the winter, you're pretty sick of it."

Mark looked toward the window. "Do you think your Alpha will come home early because of the snow? Probably not a good idea to stay out in it."

I looked down into my cup. "No."

"Will he stay in town?"

Damn it, stop asking so many questions. I gritted my teeth. "No." I tried not to be annoyed. Mark was simply curious. It was obvious I wasn't receiving any support.

His Alpha leader was coming out. He wanted to make sure I was all right. I was a pregnant Omega living in a house that was in shambles. He was just right to be worried about me.

"He's not coming home," I said.

"Away on business?"

"Mark, stop … it's not that simple."

Mark turned to face me. "I'm concerned."

"And I appreciate that."

Mark grunted and rose to his feet. He reached for and took my empty cup and headed for the kitchen. The sound of water was followed by the clatter of dishes being washed.

I tried not to feel guilty, but I appreciated the help. I hadn't perfected a technique to wash the dishes one-handed yet. The healer assured me I'd get there—adapt.

It was too much to adapt to all at once. One week after mating, we'd celebrated the fact I was pregnant. One week later, Peter was coming home, and he had spun out on the snow and collided with a tree. He would've survived that except his truck had bounced off it and careened down a ravine. He hadn't survived the tumble dryer effect of that portion of the crash.

I'd been angry and desperate for release from the pain. Spent many nights just howling in anguish. Being in the house had become too much to bear. In the short time we'd been together, we'd created a lot of memories there. Everywhere I looked, I saw Peter. I'd gone out to hunt.

I looked at my stump.

I'd met the trap a few miles out. A remnant of when there used to be humans occupying the land. I hadn't been paying attention. There had only been a light dusting of snow on it.

I sat and stared into the flames. My hand hadn't been salvageable.

Mark came out of the kitchen, drying his hands on a tea towel.

"Dishes are done."

"Mark, thank you."

He nodded toward the window. "I should get back out there."

"Your clothes should be dry."

Mark gave me the saddest smile. He knew I was hurting, and it was affecting him. My eyes rimmed with tears. Such emotion from a stranger. He was an extraordinary wolf.

"I'll go check," he said.

He walked down the hall and emerged a few seconds later, dressed in his outdoor clothes. He was an imposing wolf in sharp contrast to his demeanor. I felt safe around him.

"See you in a couple of hours to defrost again," he said.

"I'll lift some meat from the freezer for dinner before it freezes."

"Are you able to keep the fire stoked?"

"Yeah, I can manage."

"Okay." He hesitated, studying me. Then turned away. "See you in a bit."

It was a nice feeling. Knowing someone was going to be coming back to me. To sit and have dinner with me. Part of me prayed the snow would keep coming down.

It would be nice to have an Alpha wolf in the house.

Maybe I could spend one night at home without crying.

IT WAS ANOTHER THREE HOURS until Mark came into the house again. The light was fading outside. The snow wasn't stopping. They were fighting a losing battle out there.

Mark was so covered in snow that he stripped out of his coat and pants right in my front entry. I bundled everything in my arms and carried it to the dryer with him right behind me. I'd seen them finishing up outside, so I'd put the sweatpants and sweater he'd borrowed in the dryer to heat up.

He groaned, smiling as he put them on and then raced to the living room. I'd kept the fire roaring. My house was heated throughout. Even still, I found him standing facing the flames.

I'd made coffee.

"Do you want a hot coffee?"

Mark stepped closer to the flames and leaned his head against my mantel.

"That would be perfect."

"Cream and sugar?"

"Splash of cream. Three sugars."

I smiled. "So essentially candied coffee."

"Blame my sire. Started feeding me coffee at a young age. Only way I could stomach it."

"Was your sire a plumber?"

"General contractor."

"My sire too." I made my way into the kitchen and prepared Mark his coffee concoction. I brought it to him and set it on the mantel. He'd be there in front of the flames for a while yet.

I sat on the sofa and looked him over. He was my sire's age but more powerful. Everything about him was muscular. I tucked my feet up and pulled a blanket over them. Even in the heat, my feet were always cold. The sock on my stump was itchy. I pulled off the offending material.

I felt comfortable with Mark.

I looked up. He was staring at the reddened, lumpy flesh.

"It'll look better over time. Still pretty raw. Thankfully, we heal fast."

"Does it hurt?" He sat beside me; coffee forgotten.

"It throbs and aches. It's been a while since I had sharp pain."

"That must have been terrifying. Were you out on your own?"

"I was but Carina got to me pretty fast."

"Did you go to the human hospital?"

"Yeah, I needed surgery to remove my mangled hand."

I knew what his next question was, and the answer was no.

"I haven't shifted since," I said. "It would be too awkward."

"But you'll shift again someday."

I sighed and shrugged. "Probably not. Don't see the point. I can't hunt."

"To be one with your inner wolf, that's why." Mark shifted beside me and caught my gaze. "To relieve some of your sorrow. I couldn't help but notice."

My eyes were quick to tear up. Where had this sensitive wolf come from? I'd been stoic in front of everyone in my pack except Adam. Why was Mark different from my pack?

Why had I let my emotions show in front of him?

I shuddered and let my tears flow. I think I scared him a little because he jumped back in his seat. To his credit, he quickly moved closer to me and put his hand on my shoulder.

His touch put me at ease. I barely knew him, but I trusted him.

With that trust on my mind, I had a complete meltdown, ugly crying. And I didn't even feel embarrassed. Mark clamped tighter to my shoulder and caressed my tensing muscles.

He stayed with me as I cried myself out. I finally came down the other side of the mountain of grief. "I'm sorry. I didn't mean to spring that on you," I gasped.

"You needed to let that out." He squeezed my shoulder. "Stop me if I'm prying too much, but this is about more than your hand, isn't it?"

I nodded, snuffling. Mark retrieved a box of tissues for me.

"The reason my house is such a mess … I'm here alone."

"You don't have a mate?"

I shook my head. "No … I lost him 6 weeks ago."

"Oh … Reese." Mark rubbed the base of my neck. "I'm *so* sorry."

A new wave of tears and sobbing hit me. This time, Mark wrapped his arm around my shoulders and pulled me into an embrace. He leaned his cheek on the top of my head.

"I don't know what to say," he said.

"You don't need to say anything."

Just hold me.

I grabbed a second and third tissue and wiped my nose. The warmth in his grasp was different than Adam's. Mark was reacting to shocking news, holding me tighter than Adam had done.

"Can I ask what happened?"

I nodded and sighed, recovering from a sucking inhalation. "Car accident."

"The last snowstorm?"

"He spun out. Ended up down a ravine."

"Fuck, Reese." He gave my shoulders a rough rub. "Hunter told me someone had died in the pack. Left a young Omega and their unborn pup behind."

I sighed. "That would be me."

Mark gave me one last squeeze. "Stay curled up. What can I get you?"

I knew I looked a mess as he rose to his feet and looked at me. The sadness in his eyes as he studied my face was heart wrenching. Truly. Where had this caring wolf come from?

"Should I bring us some dinner?" he asked.

I exhaled and wiped the tears off my face. "That would be nice."

"Be right back."

I listened to him fussing around in the kitchen. It was a familiar sound. A sound I missed desperately. Peter had always prepared our evening meal if we had one.

This time as Mark sat beside me feeding, he didn't growl.

I used the wet dishcloth he'd brought to the coffee table to wipe my hands and face. It was nice eating in front of the fire. It fulfilled a primal part of me a little.

Maybe Mark was right. Maybe I needed to shift to relieve some of my emotions. Being in wolf form was calming, but I didn't want to be reminded of my missing paw by limping around.

Mark must have sensed my thoughts.

"Why don't you shift and lie in front of the fire," he suggested. "Get some rest."

I cradled my belly. The unending sadness in my heart was probably affecting the pup. Our pup deserved a break. Mark's encouragement was what I needed to break through my fear.

I stepped away from the sofa and removed my clothes, conscious of the fact Mark was watching me. Nudity in wolf life was nothing new. Our pack had all seen each other naked.

Mark wasn't from my pack, though, but I needed to see the warmth in his eyes as I shifted. The imbalance resulting from the missing paw caught me by surprise and I almost fell over. Mark rushed over and helped me settle on the area rug in front of the fire.

He stroked my fur until I fell asleep.

Chapter Three | Mark

I wouldn't be going home tonight. It was dark out and the snow was still coming down. Hopefully, in the morning, the weather would clear so I could call a tow truck. I'd promised my customer I would be out at her place tomorrow to work on her bathroom reno.

I looked toward the hearth. Reese's chest rose and fell slowly, his body calm without twitching or any other indication he was having nightmares. It's what he had needed. A bit of peace.

It hurt my heart to think he'd been suffering for 3 weeks without the solace of being in wolf form, but I could understand why he'd hesitated. When a human's canine had a damaged leg, the veterinarian would amputate at the shoulder so the animal could traverse with ease.

Reese needed his arm while *out of* wolf form but the weight of it would throw him off *in* wolf form. Since all wolves from our species spent more time out of wolf form, it made sense to leave the arm intact. I hadn't been surprised when he'd stumbled after shifting.

I quietly put another log on the fire and went to snoop. The cabinets in the kitchen were missing doors. And drawer fronts were absent. And the backsplash had been removed.

Reese's mate had been in mid-renovation. I wondered how far that extended. In the laundry room, the laundry sink was missing, and the cupboards were in the same state as the kitchen.

The home was a single-story bungalow. I found the main bathroom along the only hallway. The tub had been ripped out; the tiles removed. Ceramic pieces crunched beneath my feet.

Even the floor had been torn up.

I ran my hand through my hair. The house was a colossal mess. I poked my head into one of the bedrooms. There were two smaller ones, both missing carpet on the plywood floors.

The last room at the end of the hallway across from the laundry room was the owners' suite. At least it still had carpet. A bed swimming in a mound of blankets sat at its center. There were no sheets on the mattress. Reese probably couldn't put them on himself.

There was a door off to the right beyond the closet. I peered in. It was another bathroom. This one was completely renovated. Beautiful shower enclosure, stylish cabinets, sink, toilet, and fixtures. Stunning tile floor. Reese's mate had done a good job.

I was curious. I found my way to the covered carport. Stored safely were the supplies to finish the rest of the jobs. Reese's mate had left his home that morning thinking he'd be back to continue doing the renovations for his new family. His sudden death put life in perspective.

I needed to choose a mate. I'd heard there were some female Omega wolves over in West Creekside pack who might be interested in mating with a rival pack leader.

I groaned. I needed to stop dragging my feet.

I made my way back to the owners' suite, cleared the blankets off the bed, and went in search of sheets. There were some in the closet. I started with those and made the bed.

I wouldn't be disturbing Reese tonight but when tomorrow night rolled around, if he wanted to sleep in a bed, I wanted it to be done properly for him. The young wolf needed sleep.

I hauled one of the blankets I'd removed from the bed into the living room along with an extra pillow I had found in the closet. I made up a bed for myself on the sofa and climbed in.

It was still early but I was tired, and the sound of Reese sleeping was relaxing.

I pulled the blankets around me. There was a slight scent of natural soap on it. Soap and small amounts of perspiration. I inhaled, memorizing Reese's scent. I had already breathed it in as I'd held him while he cried. It was comforting. It lulled me off to sleep.

I AWOKE TO THE SOUND OF dishes clattering accompanied by swearing. Before I had a chance to jump up and help him, he wandered into the living room.

"I made some breakfast," Reese said. "Just berries and eggs."

"Perfect." I rose from the sofa and folded the blanket. I set it at one end with the pillow on top. I wouldn't be needing it again. Sunlight was streaming in through the windows.

I joined him in the kitchen and took a seat at the kitchen table. He'd laid out two bowls of mixed berries, dual tumblers with four cracked eggs each, and a cup of coffee for me.

It was nicer than what I usually made for myself. I usually scoffed some cubed roast and washed it down with a mug of coffee on the go.

"This looks good," I said.

"It's thanks for making my bed. I'll feel comfortable again. Thank you."

"I know how important rest is in your final two weeks."

"Do you have pups?"

"No." I took a sip of my coffee. The sugar ratio was perfect. "I'm not mated."

"Never?"

"I haven't found a wolf I want to be mates with."

"We have some unmated Omegas in our pack."

I nodded. "I know. Hunter told me. All males, though."

"You prefer females."

"Yeah. I heard there are some in West Creekside."

Reese wrinkled his nose.

I laughed. "What's that face for?"

"I went to school with those females. Not a fan."

"They're your age?"

"Generally."

I leaned back and crossed my arms. "How old *are* you?"

Reese finished chewing a handful of berries. "Thirty-two." He swirled the glass with the eggs in it, yellow globes amongst the albumen. "I know … late for starting pups."

"But you were waiting for your fated mate."

Reese frowned and nodded.

"Did you find him?" I asked.

"Peter … my mate."

"You loved him."

"With my whole heart." Reese swallowed the eggs in one go. He appeared to be faring better this morning. Last night, a statement like that would have led to tears. His sleep in wolf form had been restorative. I hoped he'd do it again when he was on his own.

"Your pack is here to help you raise that pup."

Reese shook his head. "I'll be all right on my own."

I hated to hear him express his reluctance to accept help from his pack. From what I knew through Hunter, East Creekside was a tight-knit pack.

"I'd like to help you."

Reese stared at me. "Why?"

"Because your pup cannot be raised amidst all this construction. And if you're *not* going to let your pack help you, maybe you'll let me. I'm removed from your life here."

I suspected that was the problem. Reese was an emotional wreck and felt guilty about losing his paw. He didn't want to feel like a burden to his pack.

His hard stare softened. "There's a lot of work to do. Are you sure?"

"It'll be a nice distraction after plumbing. I can come out on weekends."

"If you're sure you don't mind. I'd really appreciate it."

"We'll start with that bathroom. I took a look in your carport. Looks like you have everything to complete the job the same as your ensuite bathroom."

"That was the plan. To make them the same."

"Then *we* have a plan." I rose to my feet and downed the glass of eggs. The backup beeping sounds of a truck had caught my attention. "Sounds like Lucas called a tow truck already."

Reese smiled at me. "Probably wants you the hell out of here."

"Do you think I'll have trouble getting permission from him to come here every weekend?"

"No, I'll talk to him. He'll give me anything I want at this point."

"Perfect."

Reese followed me to the front door after I changed back into my own clothes in the laundry room. It was going to be a good day. It felt good. *I* felt good. Reese had brought some purpose to my life that I'd been missing. Even the tedium of today's plumbing job didn't deter that feeling.

After a long day on the job, I arrived home to an empty house. I thought back to this morning, hearing the clatter of dishes and Reese swearing in his kitchen. I longed for a sound like that in my own home. I started a fire in the fireplace. I didn't usually eat in the living room, but tonight I did.

I wondered if Reese was doing the same thing.

Wondered if he'd shift and sleep in front of the flames again.

Whether he'd find some peace.

I wanted peace for him. The best I could offer was to make his house a home again. That I could do for him. Beyond that, I didn't have much to offer him.

Nothing except—I had held him as he'd cried. I could offer him that too.

A shoulder to cry on.

I fell asleep lying on my sofa in front of the fire. At the back of my senses, Reese's scent of natural soap and perspiration drifted into my mind.

It brought *me* peace.

TWO DAYS LATER, it was the weekend. I had phoned Lucas to confirm Reese had secured permission for me to be on their territory. He made me promise to treat Reese with care. I had no other intention. The young wolf deserved to be treated with the utmost warmth.

I started out early. I wanted to get a full day in working on Reese's bathroom. I was going to finish the demo of the room, clean it up, and install the tub. I'd tackle the tile floor tomorrow. I remembered enough after helping my sire tile to do a good job.

Reese was waiting on his front porch as I pulled up to his house. He must have caught my scent as I drove close enough. It made me feel fuzzy in my stomach that he had memorized my scent. He was standing with a cup in his grasp I knew was for me.

"Morning," I said as I approached his house.

"No snow today. So that's a good thing."

"I don't need to be stranded again." Except, I had enjoyed the experience of coming into a home where someone was waiting for me. Heating my clothes in the dryer.

Curling up on the sofa to watch the flames together.

Even though Reese had spent much of our conversation in tears, I had enjoyed speaking with him. He had opened up to me. Been vulnerable. We'd made a rare connection.

I hoped a friendship would develop between us. I knew I was old enough to be his sire but there was an ease between us I enjoyed. I wanted more of that.

"That for me?" I pointed at the cup.

"One coffee with enough sugar to make the spoon stand up."

I smirked and laughed. "Thank you."

I'd had an idea overnight. I headed to the kitchen first and examined the lower cabinet next to the sink. I'd need an electrician, but it could be done.

"I'm going to install a dishwasher for you."

"Really?"

"You'll lose some cupboard space but there are only a few pots in here."

"I'll put them somewhere else. No problem. Not like I have much in the kitchen."

"I'll put in an order for one when I take a break later."

"You're a lifesaver. That'll make my life so much easier."

"Right … well, let me get to that bathroom."

Reese stepped away. "Won't hold you back."

The work was tough, removing the toilet and cabinet, and scrapping up the rest of the tile floor. I removed the light fixture and installed a single bulb I'd brought so I'd have light to work.

"Are you ready for a break?" Reese asked from behind me.

I was. I didn't have the stamina I had in my youth. I used to be able to work 10 hours straight without a break and not even feel it. Now, I could work half that and *feel* it.

"Yeah, it's a good place to stop. I'll install the tub after I rest up a bit."

"I've put out some venison cubes on the coffee table. Thought we could eat in front of the fire again. I enjoyed that. Been feeding there ever since."

I smiled. "Me too. It *was* nice."

I wasn't going to tell him how lonely I felt as I sat at home feeding alone in front of the fire. How I missed his company. How much I missed his scent.

I got comfortable on the sofa beside him. I couldn't help glancing over at him. His dark hair was longer than I kept mine. His eyebrows were thick and poised above his intense lashes.

His lashes fluttered and he turned to look at me.

"You all right?" he asked.

His pale blue eyes were mesmerizing as they watched me. My stomach did a little flip, and I was gripped with a need to touch him. I tore my attention away from him. "I'm good. Hungry. Thanks for making something. I didn't bring much. I need to head out and hunt soon."

"Lucas keeps me stocked with game."

"He's a good pack leader."

"The best." Reese gave me one of his adorable half-smiles. "I'm sure you are too."

"Aside from avoiding producing a potential heir."

"What's holding you back?"

"I have my excuses. The main one is I've been waiting for my fated mate to appear."

"That doesn't happen often in small territories like ours."

"No, I'd probably have to go to the city. Just not sure how amenable a city wolf would be to moving out into the wilderness."

"You never know. Maybe you should try."

"I'd rather sort out my life with a wolf from here."

"Well, best of luck. I don't envy you."

Not sure where it came from, but I needed to know. "Do you think you'll ever mate again?"

Reese's beautiful eyes became shadowed beneath his brow. "I like to think I will find love again. Right now, though … I need to heal."

"Of course." I cleared my throat, an inkling of disappointment tickling my insides. I didn't want to analyze what that meant beyond wanting the best for Reese. Wanting his happiness.

"Feed," Reese said and picked up a cube of meat. My inner wolf saw red and I almost cleaned the plate. Something stopped me from taking the last few cubes.

I'd never had that happen before.

My vision cleared and I pushed the plate toward Reese.

"The pup needs this."

Reese placed his hand on my knee. "Thank you."

A bit of air was sucked from my lungs as Reese released my leg. It had been a touch between friends. Except it had tied knots in my emotions. I wanted him to touch me again.

I needed to go back to work.

"I'll get to this tub." It was going to be impossible to move on my own. "I'll need a hand."

Reese snorted and laughed. "I have *one* I can offer you."

I smiled at him. It was nice to hear him lightening up. I had checked his bedroom. It didn't look like he'd been sleeping in the bed. I hoped he was shifting to wolf form to sleep.

"All right. Help me wrestle this thing into the house."

With a bit of maneuvering and swearing, we managed to relocate the tub from the carport to the bathroom. I was glad to see Reese make use of his stump to stabilize the tub. The doctor was right. In time, he would adjust. Realizing he was still capable of tasks would make all the difference. I had every confidence Reese would recover and thrive.

Reese left me alone to install the taps on the tub. Once I was done, I was going to head home. Come back early the next morning to tackle the tile flooring.

The taps done; I cleaned up my tools. I'd leave them there. No point in hauling them back and forth. Reese was flipping through a stack of papers on his kitchen table when I emerged from the bathroom. He huffed and slammed his hand on the stack.

My heart sank. He was having money problems now that his mate was gone. I knew Lucas would make up the shortfall, but Reese was probably too proud to ask.

I wasn't going to get involved.

"I'm off," I said.

Reese looked at the clock on the stove. "So soon?"

"I need a full day to start anything new."

"I appreciate everything you did today." Reese rose from his seat and walked toward me. "I enjoyed having you here. It's nice to hear the sounds of you working."

"You miss him."

"Desperately."

"We'll get your home looking the way he intended."

Tears rimmed Reese's eyes. "Thank you."

I waited to see if Reese was going to burst into tears. I wanted to be there to hold him if he did. I inhaled his scent. I'd had a dream where he had let me embrace him again.

I came close to shaking my head to dislodge the thought.

"I'll see you tomorrow," I said as I headed for the door. I was startled by Reese's hand on my shoulder, stopping me. I turned to face him. "Did I forget something?"

Reese gave me the saddest look, tears on his cheeks, and flung his arms around my shoulders. I reciprocated, wrapping my arms around him and hugging him tight.

The strength of his arms around me felt good.

"Seriously, Mark," he whispered in my ear. "Thank you."

"I'm here for you," I whispered back.

He pulled away and stepped back, sniffling. "Sorry … just needed to hug you."

"Anytime." And I meant it. Those strong arms around me had stirred something deep inside me I'd never experienced before. A feeling of completeness.

The whole drive home, I kept bringing myself to the moment I had felt as if I had unlocked something. I gripped the steering wheel. Reese had unlocked something.

I was reminded the next morning when I showed up at his house and he was waiting on his porch for me again—coffee in hand. A ripple of profound affection nearly floored me.

He flashed me a smile that lit up his eyes as I mounted the steps.

"Good morning," he said and handed me my cup. It was the same cup I had used yesterday. It had a corny *live love* slogan on it. He had washed it for me.

"It is. It's going to be a good day."

"Floor?"

"Yeah, I haven't tiled in a long time, but I should be fine."

He left me at the door to the carport. "Holler if you need any help."

It was slow going. I was glad I'd given myself an entire day to tile. Some of the cuts near the doorway were fidgety.

After a short break, I grouted the floor. It was the final step for today.

I washed my hands and tools in the kitchen sink. I'd install the laundry sink next weekend before painting the bathroom.

I found Reese in the living room; sound asleep on the sofa. He was cupping his belly as he slept. He was going to make a good carer of the pup. The thought brought out an instinct in me. I wanted to protect Reese and his pup. Beyond what I should be feeling.

I pulled a blanket over him, covered his shoulders, and added another log to the fire. His face bathed in the firelight had a warm glow. It softened his features.

He looked so serene.

I couldn't stop myself. I brushed some of the hair hanging onto his cheek away. His eyes fluttered open, and he smiled at me, sleep still keeping a soft hold on him.

"Hey," he whispered.

"Hey."

There was a silent exchange between us. My stomach fluttered, disturbing my breath. I couldn't pull my gaze away. As he looked up at me, his lips parted, I realized he felt it too.

It was time for me to go.

"I'll see you next weekend."

"I'll be here."

I headed for the door, longing for him to pull me into an embrace like yesterday. Maybe next weekend there would be an opportunity to touch him again.

I fell asleep that night thinking about how he had looked up at me with those incredible eyes. That simple *hey* had stirred my heart. The curve of his lips as he spoke it plagued my dreams.

I wanted things I shouldn't want from him.

Chapter Four | Reese

As I stirred my ginger tea, my back spasmed and then all loving hell wrapped its tendrils around my belly. The pain almost took me to my knees.

It was time.

I clambered around and gathered some towels and brought them to the bed. I was supposed to call Jonas and Adam at the onset of whelping, but I didn't want to bother them.

I could do this myself.

I stripped out of my clothes, settled on the bed, and another contraction hit. I rolled onto my hand, stump, and knees to relieve the pressure on my back. I steadied my breathing, not wanting to hyperventilate. I didn't have much of a reprieve until the next one barreled through me.

I groaned and screamed as the next wave of pain put imaginary claws in my belly.

"Reese?"

Mark rushed in, his eyes scanning the room. His presence barely registered. I was concentrating on catching my breath. I'd been about to make coffee for his arrival.

"Is the pup coming?"

I sucked in a gasp and nodded my head.

"Should you call someone?"

I shook my head. "No. Do it myself."

"Nonsense, Reese. Call out to them."

I didn't want a bedroom full of Omega wolves, all doting on me. Wolfs had been whelping on their own for countless centuries. I shook my head.

"Stubborn." Mark climbed onto the edge of the bed. "What can I do?"

"Massaging my back would be amazing."

"That I can do." Mark's big warm hands smothered my spine and he caressed and applied pressure to my aching muscles. He moved closer to me to perfect his technique.

I groaned.

It felt *so* good.

Then the clenching agony started again. I screamed and almost fell over as my weight shifted toward my stump. The position was no longer working for me.

I lowered myself onto my side, forcing Mark to move back. One of his hands had shifted from my back to my waist, where it still sat. I closed my eyes and soaked in the attention as Mark's hand drifted to my sore belly. My comfort was complete as he lay down behind me.

"I'm right here for you," he whispered against my ear, his breath warm and so welcome.

I was about to speak when another contraction had me swearing and clenching the sheets. Mark caressed my belly through the entirety of it.

We lay together through each contraction, Mark at my back, breathing with me, his gentle hand on my belly. The leader of the Riverton pack was everything I needed.

The overall feeling of my body changed, making me slightly crazed. My body became desperate to expel the pup. The urge was unstoppable. "I need to push."

"Do I need to do anything?"

"Hold me. Remind me to breathe."

I bent my arm intending to reach for his hand, forgetting I didn't have one. Instead, Mark enveloped my stump with his hand and clung to it.

During the next contraction, I bore down as Mark held me tight against him.

"Breathe," he reminded me.

A few more pushes and I could feel the pup breach my hole. I was almost there. I inhaled the scent of Mark and memorized the feel of him holding me.

"One more," I said.

"You're doing amazing."

One last contraction and the pup slipped out. I was quick to sit up and grab a towel. I was rough as I rubbed the pup's fur. I lifted it and blew into its mouth and nose.

Its little body wriggled, and it let out the most gorgeous mewl.

I lifted its backend. He was a male. I inhaled his aroma. Omega.

"He's beautiful," Mark said beside me. He crowded against my back so he could get a better look. "Exquisite silky black fur like yours."

My heart had never felt so full. I put my pup's little black nose against my lips and kissed him. My tears fell onto his fur. My love for Peter had been eclipsed by this miracle of ours.

"I'm going to name him Peter."

"I think that's fitting." Mark brushed his hand over my hair. "I'll leave you alone with him."

"Thank you." I touched his arm with my stump. "For everything."

"It was an honor to be with you."

Mark was quiet as he left the room. Even closing the door without a sound. I tidied up the afterbirth, lay on the damp bedding, brought my pup close, and shifted.

The tiny being found his way to me to suckle. I fell asleep to the pull of his mouth and the sound of him sucking. And the memory of Mark holding me.

THERE WAS A LIGHT TAPPING on the door. I lifted my head, ready to protect my pup. I relaxed as Mark peered around the edge of the door.

I sneezed and inhaled to get a good draw of his scent. It was more complex in wolf form. I could smell his soap, his toothpaste, the meat he'd ingested, and his perspiration.

"I've finished installing the laundry sink and wiping the dry grout off the tile floor. Halfway through tiling the tub enclosure. I'm trying to do quiet things."

I blinked at him.

"I'm going to stay here tonight in case you need anything."

My brow dipped and I whined. He didn't need to do that. He'd done enough for me today. I hadn't expected to have a whelping coach. I'm glad it was Mark.

"I'll get you some water and something to eat."

He left the door open. The heat and smell of burning cedar drifted in from the living room. I might feel more comfortable out there. Peter was asleep. I moved away and shifted.

I washed my body at the sink and pulled on some easy comfortable sweat clothes. I lifted the pup with one hand and cradled him against my chest. I inhaled the scent on the top of his head.

"Smell his head," I said to Mark as I entered the kitchen where he was preparing some meat. Mark put the knife down and obliged, sniffing little Peter's furry head.

"Smells like a miracle."

I smiled. "He does, doesn't he."

When he was this close, Mark's gentle brown eyes made you feel like everything would be right in the world if you let him in.

I cleared my throat and went into the living room to cozy up. It was becoming a habit, eating in front of the fireplace. Mark deposited a plate with strips of steak on it on the coffee table.

Peter started to fuss. He'd be feeding first. I decided to try chest feeding rather than shifting. I was comfortable where I was. "Can you hold him for a second?"

With two hands, Mark cupped the pup like he was as breakable as fine china. I stripped off my sweatshirt. My nipples were puffy and leaking. Mark placed Peter in my crooked right arm, and I directed the pup to one. I was able to stroke his fur with my left hand as he fed.

Mark lifted the plate toward me. I took a strip of steak and put it in my mouth. It tasted better than it had in weeks. Whatever had been making me feel nauseous had cleared from my system.

I took three more and stuffed them in my mouth. It wasn't until I was chewing that I realized Mark hadn't taken any yet. He'd fed an Omega first. My heart jumped in my chest.

Maybe it was the euphoric chemicals circulating through my body, but I felt compelled to lean against him, shoulder to shoulder. He hugged me to him and kissed the side of my head.

"You and the pup are a picture of beauty," Mark said.

"Thank you."

"Today was a very good day."

I smiled. "It was." I snuggled closer to Mark. "I'm glad you shared it with me."

"Because you're stubborn."

I laughed softly so as not to disturb Peter. "I've been told that."

"Have you told them now? Your Omega's?"

"Adam knows. He'll be over later."

Mark kissed my head again. "I'm glad you shared it with me too."

I tickled the pup's belly to keep him suckling. "Uncle Mark."

I said it but it didn't feel quite right. The way Mark was holding me and kissing my head, there was more going on. Not sure I was ready. I'd only been a widow for 2 months.

His warmth felt good against me.

Mark stroked Peter's head and then touched my chin. He turned my face to him.

"I don't want to take advantage," he said. "Your emotions are running high."

I felt a surge of need spinning up from my gut.

I closed the gap before he had a chance to speak again. I wanted those lips on mine. I crushed my mouth against his. He was quick to respond, chasing what I was offering.

We ended the kiss when Peter squeaked and whined, and stretched out his little legs, yawning. Mark kissed my cheek as we watched him fall asleep.

Mark hoisted himself away from me. "I going to get back to my tiling job before the glue dries out. Then I'll get Adam to help me bring in the cabinet when he gets here."

I liked how Mark could move from tenderness to practicality. He had the heart of a teddy bear but the work ethic of a locomotive. Work needed to be done, but his mood might easily shift back the other way. There was a quick knock on the door, then a blast of cold air, announcing Adam's arrival. "Let me see him." Adam sat on the sofa beside me and held out his hands.

I transferred the sleeping bundle.

"He has beautiful fur." Adam stroked him along his spine. "He looks healthy."

"He has a good appetite."

"You're not having any trouble feeding?"

"None."

"Are you bleeding still?"

"I put on one of those pads you gave me."

Adam sniffed Peter's head. "I love that smell. Sometimes I wonder if that's the only reason I keep having them. It's like an addiction."

"I've named him Peter."

"Oh … that's wonderful." Adam passed Peter back to me. He was still small enough to fit in one hand. I wasn't sure what I was going to do as he got older and bigger.

Adam looked toward the bathroom. "Mark stayed with you the whole time?"

"Didn't leave me alone for a second."

"Lucas says he's an unusual Alpha. Soft as muck on the inside."

"So is Lucas."

Adam tipped his head. "True."

I wasn't sure if I should tell him. I didn't know if it was leading anywhere or if we had just shared a moment of emotion because of the pup. I decided to wait. The kiss was private between Mark and me. There was no guarantee that it would happen again.

"I should leave you to rest. Don't let Mark make any noise."

"He won't. I think he wants you to help him with the bathroom cabinet before you go."

"I'll do that and leave by the carport." He leaned down and kissed my head. "Your pup is gorgeous. Call me if you have any questions."

"Will do." I set the pup in my lap as Adam conferred with Mark and they went outside to bring in the cabinet. I laughed listening to them. Adam swore worse than I did.

I stretched out my arms. I was sore and tired. I needed my bed. I gathered up little Peter and found the high-sided flannel pup bed Jonas had given me and curled up on my side on my mattress with the circular foam bed at my belly. My body was close enough to keep him warm.

I pulled a blanket over our entirety.

The mattress dipped behind me, and I looked over my shoulder.

"Is it all right if I join you?" Mark asked, already partway on the bed.

"Please."

Mark snuggled up behind me and draped his arm over me. His hand snuck up my arm and gripped the remnants of my wrist as gently as a feather.

He kissed the back of my neck.

"I'm here for you, Reese," he whispered. "You and the pup."

I rolled onto my back, and he rose on one elbow, hovering over me.

"Please don't hurt me," I whispered.

Mark's eyebrows pinched together. "Never, Reese. I'd never hurt either of you."

"My heart is fragile right now."

"We don't have to go beyond what we're doing. I just need to be near you."

I couldn't help it. The tears started flowing. I wanted to be near him too. I wanted his warm arms around me. His lips on mine. I just wasn't sure I was ready for a relationship.

I reached for his face and pulled him to me. He set the most tender kiss on my lips and then pulled away and wiped the tears from my cheeks.

"Sleep. We'll talk later."

I turned back on my side and Mark cupped me as if we were always meant to fit together. Hot breath at the back of my neck, his hand on my hip, his foot caressing mine.

It was the perfect ending to a perfect day.

THE SMELL OF COFFEE woke me. Peter was still sleeping. I gathered him up in the pup bed and brought him to the living room. I set the bed a safe distance from the fire.

I went into the kitchen. Mark was arranging mixed berries in two bowls along with glasses of raw eggs. He turned to look at me and smiled.

"Good morning, Reese."

I wanted his arms around me again. I wandered up to him, close enough that he knew what I needed. He wrapped me up in his arms. I clung to him and tucked my nose against his shoulder.

"Good morning," I mumbled into his sweater.

I stepped back and held his face. One hand and one stump. He didn't flinch in the slightest. His breaths came out short and shallow. He was waiting for me to make the first move.

I kissed him, long and lingering; our tongues yearning for more. His mouth tasted of the berries he'd snuck from the bowls. I parted from his lips and pressed my forehead to his.

"Please, can we take this slow?" I asked.

"Absolutely. I've never done this before."

"Wanting to be near a male?"

"It's never happened before." Mark brushed his fingers along my temple. "My age doesn't bother you? I'm old enough to be your sire."

I shook my head. "I don't care."

"I feel a strong desire to protect you and Peter."

"I feel safe with you."

Mark captured another kiss from my lips. He smiled as he stepped away. "Do you want meat with your breakfast?"

"I should. And a glass of water. That pup is draining me dry."

"Sit. I'll bring everything to you."

I pulled out a kitchen chair, took a seat, and let Mark wait on me. It was endearing how he fussed over me. Peter had never been this attentive. I looked down at my bowl.

I missed him. His smile. His jokes and ability to make me laugh.

And how much he loved me.

My heart ached.

Mark put his hand on my stump. "Are you all right?"

"Just thinking about Peter. Senior."

"Do you want to stop what we're doing?"

I gazed into his gentle eyes. "No, but I have a lot to process still."

"You're not ready." Mark sighed. "I'm sorry. I shouldn't have pushed you."

I frowned. He hadn't. I'd made the first move by leaning against him. I'd accepted the hug and the kisses on my head. I'd launched myself at his lips.

"You haven't pushed me. We were on a path to each other. The timing isn't great, but I need you in my life. Not just for the support. I think we have something special happening."

"I feel it too." He brushed his thumb back and forth over my mangled wrist. My disability didn't turn him off at all. He'd been shocked at first but now he accepted me as me.

That felt amazing.

Little Peter started squeaking in the living room. I finished what I could of the food before dashing out to attend to him. He was predictably hungry again. I wiped his tiny bottom first with a disposable toilette to stimulate and clean him. He squealed at me. Angry I was taking so long.

I lifted off my sweatshirt and latched him on. The dropping sensation behind my nipples always caught me off guard. My uncovered one started leaking.

Mark sat beside me to watch me feed Peter.

His attention was apt as he watched with fascination. If we were further in our relationship, I'd have asked him to play with my other nipple. It was itching for attention.

I bent toward him and stole another kiss instead. It would have to do for now. We'd agreed to take our developing relationship slow. Mark was out of his depth, having never been attracted to a male before. It must be messing with his head. And I hadn't finished mourning.

Mark rose from the sofa and walked behind it. "I'm going to install the toilet and sink today and clean up. The bathroom will be done in an hour or so. We can run you a nice bath to soak in."

I turned on the sofa so I could see him. "That's going to be amazing not having to use the ensuite all the time. When Peter gets bigger, I'll be able to wash him in a proper tub."

I looked at my stump. How on earth was I going to do that?

Mark interpreted my sudden deflation. "We'll figure it out together."

I simply nodded. Mark wasn't going to be around all the time. I'd need to figure a lot of this stuff out on my own. I cleared my mind. I was looking forward to a bath.

Mark had already seen my nude body twice.

Maybe I could get him to wash my back.

Chapter Five | Mark

This weekend, I was tackling the kitchen. Luckily, Reese's late mate had already painted the cabinets and cabinet doors. I just needed to install them and affix some handles. I'd cut out the portion of the cupboard to size so I could install the dishwasher that had arrived during the week.

Lucas had come over and wired the back of the cut out area with an electrical outlet while I wasn't there. Reese thought it was best to not have me in the house when other wolves came over in case they caught us staring at each other with absolute affection in our eyes.

He'd asked me if he could call me every night after he put little Peter down for a nap. He phoned between dinner and bedtime. Different times, although he was getting the pup accustomed to a feeding schedule so Reese knew when he could get some sleep himself.

We'd been talking for over an hour every night.

I reclined in my office chair as the phone rang. I picked it up.

"Hey, you." I knew it was him. Who else would be phoning me at night?

"Hey."

"How's Peter today?"

"Growing fast. Adam says he's doing great. I'm looking forward to him opening his eyes soon. I want to see what color they are."

"I hope they're pale blue like yours."

"Peter's were green. They might be green."

"That would be wonderful too. Eyes like his sire."

There was silence on the line.

"Are you thinking about him a lot today?" I asked.

"He keeps popping in. He'd be pleased with what you did with the bathroom."

"I just installed what he'd already picked out."

Another pause.

"I was wondering if you'd come tonight instead of tomorrow."

It was Friday night. I hadn't planned on going to Reese's until the morning. I wasn't sure what his intentions were. Would I be able to fall asleep with him in my arms again?

Or would he want to keep some distance and just talk.

That question was answered when I arrived at his house ninety minutes later. Reese hung his arms around my neck and caressed his lips onto mine.

I growled, clung to him, backed him against the wall, and deepened the kiss. He responded, moaning into my mouth, and raked his hand into my hair, holding me to him.

Peter fussed in his pup bed, mewling.

Reese laughed against my lips. "I'm taking a rain check on the rest of that kiss."

"I'll hold onto it for you."

I adjusted my pants as I hightailed it to the kitchen to be out of sight of Reese. My cock had never gotten hard for a male before. That kiss, though. It had undone me.

I needed to come to terms with a couple of things. It was a natural option for two males to form a mated pair among our species. That's why Omega males could become pregnant. But it was never something I'd ever considered. I enjoyed the company and the bodies of females.

Reese, though … he'd done something to my heart and my body.

Contentious item number two. I was terrified I was running straight into a serious bout of heartache. Reese was right. Our timing was all wrong. He was still grieving.

From the first day I'd met him, I knew there was something special about Reese. Spending time with him in his home and all the hours we'd talked on the phone confirmed that.

Reese was a genuine, passionate ... and stubborn wolf. His levels of passion ranged from pack politics to his diet, to wanting the best for his pup ... to his ability to love deeply.

He had loved his fated mate, Peter. So desperately, it broke my heart when he told me brief snippets about their lives together. He tried not to talk about him, but sometimes Peter was on his mind. He'd need to unload before we could continue our conversation.

Each night, Reese talked about him less and less. I hoped that meant his heart was healing. I wanted the world for Reese. His laughter was something I had come to cherish.

My cock calmed and I headed to the living room. Reese had shifted to wolf form and was stretched out on his side in front of the fire, the pup happily feeding. His sleek black fur glistened in the firelight. I sat near his head, and he lifted it and put it on my lap.

I started at his muzzle and petted him right to the tips of his ears. I kept doing that until he closed his eyes. I stroked under his chin and along his neck to his chest and then went back to his face.

I laughed quietly as he started snoring.

I leaned my back against the coffee table and enjoyed the moment. Fire burning. Reese asleep on my lap. Little Peter feeding. It was sublime. My heart soared.

This is what life was supposed to feel like.

This was a good day.

After an hour, Reese stirred. He lifted his head and pulled himself away from his pup. After taking an awkward few steps, he shifted.

This time, seeing his bare skin brought on different emotions. Especially, in the firelight. His flesh was glowing amber. I rose to my feet, enthralled. His muscles were beautiful. He was built like a weightlifter. Thick arms and legs; his belly still puffy from carrying the pup.

His cock—long and thick. It made my desire for him stir.

He was slow but Reese put on his clothes as he studied my expression.

"Should we go to bed?" Reese asked.

"Yeah, I'm tired."

"Can you gather up little Peter? I'll meet you in there."

I watched him walk down the hall. Even as bulky as he was, Reese was graceful. My heart thundered around in my chest. He was pure male wolf.

And I was falling hard for him.

I gathered up Peter, enjoying the squeaks because I had disturbed him. I could already tell; he was going to be a handful. I placed him in the pup bed and carried him to Reese's bedroom.

Reese was already stretched out on the bed, almost asleep.

I put the pup bed at his belly, covered them both with a blanket, and climbed in behind Reese.

He hummed as I snuggled up against him.

I kissed the base of his neck. He hummed again. I took it further, peeling his sweatshirt away so I could lick and suck near the claiming area between his neck and shoulder.

He moaned and reached back for me with his stump. It came to rest on my neck. I turned my head and kissed the inside of his arm. A row of kisses one after the other until I reached the angry flesh of his stump. I kissed it gently. Its absence was as much a part of him as anything else.

Reese.

The wolf who was throwing my carefully constructed life on its head.

I needed to slow it down. My cock was hard and throbbing.

I kissed his earlobe. "Sleep."

"Please hold me," Reese replied.

"All night." I gripped him to me, not caring that my stiff cock was jammed against his back. He wouldn't be surprised by what he had done to me.

My sleep was broken. Every time Reese stirred to feed Peter, I was dragged from my dreams of him. The reality was always better.

"Sorry I keep waking you," he said.

I smiled and kissed the back of his head. "I don't mind. I like listening to Peter feed. All his little grunts and slurps are adorable."

"He really is perfect."

So are you.

I couldn't say it aloud. It was too soon. The last thing I wanted to do was rush Reese. I was even second-guessing sucking on his neck. I had to remind myself that he would've stopped me if it was too much. I was going to wait and let him make the next move … if there was one.

I was surprised when the sun streaming through the draperies woke me. I tucked my face against the base of Reese's neck, inhaled the scent of him, and tugged him close.

Sometime during the night, he'd removed his sweatshirt and thrown the blankets off. It probably made feeding easier. He groaned and pressed his ass against my sleepy cock.

It soon woke up as he ground against it.

Reese rolled onto his back and then onto his right side. He cupped my face and kissed me, then played with the curls of greying hair at my temples.

"Very distinguished," he said.

"Old."

Reese smiled at me. "Not to me." It had kept me up on a couple of nights over the past week. If I was too old for Reese. Why would a young wolf like Reese be interested in me? I was nothing special. I was a good leader. Direct, loyal, honest, fair, and organized.

That's all I had going for me.

Reese touched my bottom lip and then dragged it down. He traced his finger down my chin and along my throat to my collarbone. Slowly down my chest to my stomach.

"Kiss me," he whispered as his hand busied itself undoing my pants.

I complied, too far gone to do anything except what he asked of me. Reese tucked his hand behind the waistband of my underwear and grasped my cock. His fingers were rough and thick. I closed my eyes and groaned, a hunger and satisfaction I thought would redefine me instead bringing my life into focus. There was a rightness in the feel of his hand.

Reese edged closer, sinking deeper into my mouth with his tongue. He had my cock hard now. His palm swept up and down my shaft while I rocked my hips. His thumb rubbed over my slit, spreading the precum over my cockhead. He moved even closer.

I just about went into a tailspin as his sweatpant-covered, hard cock pressed against mine. He released my cock and struggled between us, presumably hauling his pants off his hips.

Bliss. Complete bliss as his silky cock brushed across mine, and then pressed against my length. He took both of our cocks in his hand and stroked them together in his palm.

We both grunted as he worked, fast—slow, hard—soft. Reese attacked my mouth as he increased the intensity of his hand. He pistoned his hips, his mouth frantic.

I met him in his frenzy.

My hand was all over him. Raking through his hair, gripping his face, clawing at his back—grasping his ass and encouraging him.

Reese gasped, tipped his head back, and shuddered. His hand began slipping freely over my cock, our skin slicked by his seed. The sensation had me grasping his ass as I filled his hand.

Our bodies bucked as Reese's hand slowed. He pulled at my bottom lip with his teeth, then laughed, and kissed my chin. "Well, that was unexpected."

"A first for me."

"And you liked it?"

I laughed. "What do you think?" I shuffled away from him. "I'll get us a towel."

I stumbled off the bed, my legs like jelly, and headed for the ensuite. I grabbed a towel, wiped off my abdomen and cock, and came back to Reese. He cleaned his cock as I climbed back onto the bed. Watching him wipe its length brought on a sense of deep longing.

I groaned under my breath as my mouth watered.

I wanted things from his body that he might never be ready to share with me.

I kneeled on the bed and cleaned our combined seed from his hand. His palm. And finger by finger. He was facing me as I lay down, pants around his knees. His teats were leaking, little beads of white dripping onto the bedding. I licked my lips as he played with one rosy puffy nipple.

Fixing his gaze on me, Reese released his nipple and transferred his fingers to my lips. I opened my mouth, and he slipped them inside. The taste was unusual. I'd become familiar with the scent of his milk. The intricacies of it mixed with a hint of seed danced differently on my tongue.

I closed my lips around his fingers and sucked. Reese moaned and pushed them further inside my mouth. I swirled my tongue around his thick fingers and slicked them up.

Reese gasped as he slid his fingers out and I tickled the ends of them with my tongue.

"Mark." His voice was rough and quiet. There was a new desire in his eyes. I knew what he was asking me. What he needed from me.

All he had to do was ask. I would give Reese anything he needed or wanted. I kissed his lips and then his chin. My heart danced around as I kissed the side of his neck and he rolled onto his back. I spent some time there, tasting his skin, wallowing in the essence of him.

Across his collarbone, peppering him with my lips. Down the center of his chest to his soft warm belly. It wouldn't be long until it was rock hard again.

Then I descended to a region I had never thought I'd find myself in. I grasped his hardening cock in one hand. It was substantial. The scent was overwhelming. A mixture of our combined seed and his precum. I tasted there first. Reese's hips bucked and he gasped as I tongued his slit.

He tasted briny. Clean and so incredibly virile. I pulled his foreskin tight against his body and sucked in the end of his cock. It felt smooth and beautiful against my tongue.

I bobbed up and down, introducing more and more of it into my mouth until his cockhead was hitting the base of my tongue. It was difficult not to gag but I held the response at bay.

His hand raked into my hair.

"Oh … Mark," he whispered. The base of his cock pulsed against my tongue, and he flooded my throat, causing me to concentrate on accepting and keeping it all.

I wanted every last drop.

I kept his cock in my mouth until it started to soften, then released it to fall spent on his thigh. I rubbed my thumb along its length. I'd just had a mind-blowing, life-changing experience.

I rushed back to his lips. Our tongues tumbled and surged as Reese sought out the remnants of what I had drawn from his body. It was an erotic end to our encounter.

Little Peter was fussing.

"I need a shower before I feed him," Reese said. "Can you mind him?"

"Let me wash my hands first." I jumped off the bed, feeling invigorated. I'd sucked a cock and it had been sublime. Reese followed me, started the shower, and stepped in.

After scrubbing my hands well, I went back to the bed. Peter was rolling back and forth, whining, looking for a teat to feed from. The best I could offer him was a finger. I lifted him from the pup bed, tucked him against my chest, and offered him my pinky.

He was content for a few seconds until he realized it wasn't providing him with the nourishment he was seeking. He prodded and pushed against my chest with his front paws and complained at the top of his voice each time he released my finger from his suckling mouth.

I leaned down and kissed his head.

I could fill a household with that scent, and it wouldn't be enough.

Reese appeared at the ensuite doorway in the nude. I instantly wanted him again. He was beautiful as he strode toward the bed. He lay facing me. He waited as Peter mewled.

He was waiting for me.

I lifted the pup and brought him to a nipple and held him until he latched on and started sucking. It was a magical thing to witness, Reese's body providing for him.

Reese cupped Peter's little backend, keeping him in place, and closed his eyes.

It was time for me to get up.

I used the main bathroom to shower and brush my teeth with a toothbrush I had brought. I wanted to install the dishwasher today after putting the kitchen cupboard doors and drawers back.

I'd do the backsplash tiles some other time.

I started with the drawers. Peter had taken the faces off to paint them. I searched his workbench and found some wooden templates to place the handles correctly. He'd even numbered the doors. It was like putting a puzzle together. I stepped back to examine my handiwork after they were all placed and hung. It made a difference not being able to see the mess of dishes.

I had just put on a pot of coffee when there was a knock at the door.

It felt weird, but I answered it.

On the doorstep, a very young Alpha male. Couldn't be more than nineteen. He frowned at me. It seemed he hadn't heard I was working on Reese's house.

"Who are you?"

"Mark Cooper."

"The leader of Riverton pack?"

"That would be me."

I stepped back when he looked as though he was going to barrel past me. He scanned the living room, then paced into the kitchen. He looked annoyed that he hadn't found Reese.

"What are you doing here?" he asked next.

"Helping Reese finish the renovation jobs his late mate started."

The young wolf inhaled and glared at me. He'd obviously detected the scent of seed.

"You're here really early."

I sighed. There was no point lying to him. He'd figured out I was doing more than working on renovations. There was so much similarity, this wolf had to be Reese's brother.

"I stayed the night."

The wolf grunted. "Swooping in before he's even healed."

"It's not like that."

He crossed his arms. "My brother isn't ready."

"That's for him to decide."

Then Reese's brother dared to growl at me. Me. The Alpha leader of a pack. Even with the age difference, I could put him down. He had to know that.

He was protective and fierce.

I liked him.

"I assure you; we are going at Reese's speed."

Reese stepped up behind me and wrapped his stubby arm around my waist, his chin on my shoulder, the pup at my back. "Back down, Harlan. He's harmless. And he's been more than respectful of my feelings. You have nothing to worry about."

"It's too soon," Harlan said.

"Not for you to judge." Reese kissed my shoulder.

"Stubborn," Harlan mumbled. "Let's see this pup of yours."

Reese walked out from behind me and passed Peter to Harlan. It was obvious Harlan had never handled a pup before.

Reese stayed close, ready to intervene if Harlan was close to dropping him. I was in awe of how protective Reese was over his pup. I was honored he trusted me with him as much as he did. He'd left me to gather up little Peter and bring him to bed last night.

"What's his name?"

"Peter."

Harlan nodded as he stroked the pup's spine. "Good name." He lifted his gaze and stared at me. "I'm not convinced *he's* a good idea. You're vulnerable. You've just whelped."

Reese sighed. "Stop being such an Alpha, little brother. You're not winning this one."

"Carina isn't going to be happy about you rutting with a rival pack's leader."

"Then she'll be really upset that it's more than rutting."

"More?"

"Mark and I have become close."

"And where is this going to lead? Are you planning to join his pack? Move away from your family? I said you should have moved back into Carina's house after Peter died."

I wanted to speak but I knew it wasn't my place. I wanted to tell Harlan how much I cared for his brother. To explain what he was doing to my heart. That he was slowly becoming my world.

As for where it was leading? I hadn't thought that far ahead. I was still in shock that any of this was happening. Reese and I needed to have a conversation.

"I have a dishwasher to install," I said.

"Yes," Reese replied. "Let's go to the living room, Harlan." He took Peter back into his safe hand, resting his furry little body against his chest. "Leave Mark to his work."

After a few adjustments to the plumbing, and some grunting and swearing, I slid the dishwasher into place. I pushed the start button, and it fired up with the welcome sound of water. I'd need to pick up some dishwasher detergent for Reese. I'd head into town later and buy some.

I had tried not to listen to Reese and his brother, but it was impossible to shut out what was being said. The living room was right off the kitchen. Harlan had a million questions about me. Some Reese was able to answer. Others not. We were still getting to know each other.

Reese told his brother that what he had discovered about me warmed his heart. That he was serious about his feelings for me and that they weren't just a response to his loneliness, something else I had obsessed about during my sleepless nights.

Maybe that was the only reason Reese was interested in me.

He was lonely.

I was handy.

I washed my hands in the sink. It felt like more than that. I knew where my heart was leading me. I was tumbling fast. Now that we'd been intimate, it brought what we were doing to a whole new level. There was promise and possibility. Reese wasn't just a friend I occasionally crossed boundaries with by holding him as he slept. Reese had initiated a significant step.

This was more than loneliness.

I was sure of it.

A rush of cold air and the front door closed. Harlan had left. Reese was mine again. I wanted him all to myself. I found him in the living room, staring at the cold fireplace.

"Fire?" I asked.

"Please."

I collected some small tinder and built a nest atop some strips of birch bark. I lit it and waited until the flame had taken well before adding some logs.

I sat on the sofa beside Reese.

"We need to talk," he said.

I put my hand on his knee. "I agree."

"What *are* we doing?" He kissed the top of Peter's head. "I've been widowed for less than three months. Maybe we *are* moving too fast."

"Does it feel too fast?"

Reese shook his head. "It feels like it was fated."

"Are you enjoying what's unfolding?"

Reese looked at me with tears in his eyes. "It feels right." He swiped away a tear that escaped onto his cheek with his stump. "But where is what's happening between us going to lead?"

"Do you see yourself falling in love again?"

It was a bold question, but I needed to know how open Reese was to loving again.

Reese's brow furrowed. "My heart is still aching, but I hope I'll find love again. Before Peter, I didn't know how deeply I could love another wolf. I learned things about myself."

"You're very loving. And you're fierce about that love. I see it when you look at your pup."

Reese exhaled long and slow. "Let's take this one day at a time. I can't promise I won't change my mind. The thought of someday leaving my family is difficult for me to process."

"I won't pressure you to do anything you don't want to do."

"I know. I know that about you. I trust you."

At least the trust was there. But so much uncertainty. My heart would need to brace itself for a day when Reese might pull away. In the meantime, I planned to enjoy every moment I had with him. I would soak in every glorious minute as my affection grew.

One day at a time.

Reese held my face and kissed me. My heart skittered forward, taking another step toward an emotion completely foreign to me. This was going to hurt. Deep in my soul, I knew it.

This was going to hurt.

Chapter Six | Reese

I insisted on going into town with Mark. I was going crazy wandering around my house all day and night. I needed to see something different. Anything at all.

We were starting with a midday meal at *Growlers*. Jonas' diner. I couldn't remember the last time I'd eaten out. Peter had always preferred to eat at home.

We were in luck; the back booth was vacant. We took a seat, and I checked on little Peter. I had bundled him up in a knit sweater and a woolen blanket, then placed him in a soft plush contraption that wrapped around my body and cradled Peter against my chest.

He was toasty and asleep.

"Well, well ...." Jonas approached our booth. "Glad to see you out, Reese. Too much alone time does stuff to your head." He looked at Mark. "Mark. A pleasure to see you. Lucas tells me you're doing some renovation work for Reese. Finishing up some projects."

"Almost finished the kitchen today. Just the backsplash left."

"Nice."

"Going to tackle the bedrooms next. Give them a fresh coat of paint. Peter had picked some linoleum for the floors in there for pups. Might have to bring someone in to install it."

I smiled. Mark was rambling. Jonas was making him nervous. I decided to break the tension and reached across the table for Mark's hand. Harlan knew about us which meant everyone would know in time. I counted the seconds, wondering if he'd take me up on my offer.

He slipped his hand into mine and squeezed it.

"So, it's true," Jonas said. "You two are an item."

It seemed that Harlan had already spread the news. I'd shut out the chatter of my wolf pack, wanting to fully enjoy my pup and Mark's company. I'd missed the announcement.

"We're trying it on for size," I said.

"Looks adorable from where I'm standing. Roasts?"

"Too much food," I replied. "I'll have a flank steak and a glass of water."

"Are the roasts raw?" Mark asked.

"Fresh from the butcher this morning."

"I'll take one. Cut in quarters."

I knew why he was asking for the roast to be cut. He was planning on slipping some pieces onto my plate, encouraging me to eat more. My appetite had been funny since the whelping.

I slid my foot along his leg as Jonas turned from the table. Mark smiled at me. It was a smile that fired up familiar emotions in me it was so innocent and unsure.

"You're adorable," I said to him.

"Never heard that one before."

"There's a gentleness about you that is downright edible." I bit my lower lip as I watched him studying me. Again, to that feeling. "Where in the world did you come from?"

Mark laughed. "Riverton?"

"No, tell me about your upbringing." I rubbed his calf with my toe and clung tighter to his hand. "I've told you everything about me."

I had. I'd probably bored him. My sire had found two female Omega mates. The first chosen mate had produced me. His second and fated mate had produced my brother. It had been interesting having two carriers in the house. They couldn't have been more different from each other.

Harlan's carrier had been fun and carefree and used to let me get away with stuff as a teenager that would have sent my own carrier into an angry fit. Neither of us had inherited many traits from our carriers. We were both like our sire. Serious. Loyal. Protective.

My sire and his two mates had moved to be part of his fated mate's pack when Harlan turned sixteen and shifted. They'd left my younger brother in my hands to care for. I'd become a sire of sorts overnight. We'd shared a bedroom in Carina's house until I met Peter.

I'd filled Mark in on all of it.

"Not much to tell," Mark said. "I take after my sire. He was the leader of the pack before me. Pretty sure the gentleness comes him, but my carrier was very soft and attentive."

"Where are they?"

"They chose to live outside the pack when I took over. My sire was anxious to have a bit of solitude after being the leader for forty years."

"Do you have siblings?"

"One Alpha brother, Declan. Much younger."

"Does he live in your compound?"

"No, he's off in the city chasing a career outside construction."

"What does he do?"

Mark smiled at me. "He's an accountant."

I snorted and laughed. "I suppose that's handy."

"He is *so* boring. Always was. No fun—even when he was growing up."

I released Mark's hand as Jonas arrived with our meat. He set the plates in front of us. My steak was good and bloody. I lifted it, my canines descended, and I tore into the tasty flesh.

As I'd suspected he would, Mark deposited a quarter of his roast onto my plate.

Peter whined, the scent of the blood rousing him. Another 6 weeks and we'd be introducing him to pureed meats. I pulled myself away from feeding and looked at Mark.

We'd be introducing him to pureed meats.

Not I.

I didn't want to analyze where my mind had led me. I let myself see red and continued my feed. Jonas would watch out for me. So would Mark when he was finished.

Peter and I were safe.

I was wiping my face and fingers when the little tinkling bell attached to the front door rang and a familiar scent wafted. It had been a matter of time until she tracked me down after Harlan had filled the entire pack in on my current attraction to Mark.

I looked up. "Carina."

"Reese." She batted at my shoulder to make me move over so she could sit beside me. I had lived in Carina's house with her for fourteen years. She knew me better than anyone.

She leaned toward me and peeled back the folds of the pup snuggie. She cooed at Peter as she tickled his perfect head. He squawked and groaned. I'd need to feed him soon.

"You've named him Peter," she said.

"I did."

"That's a beautiful thing to do." She rubbed my arm. "How are you coping?"

"I'm doing well." I smiled at Mark. "Mark has been amazing."

"I heard." She stared at Mark. "Maybe a little *too* amazing."

"We're not just rutting," I clarified.

"I know. That wouldn't be like you." She leaned back and crossed her arms. "As you can imagine, Mark, I'm very protective over this young wolf. He moved in with me when he was 18."

"I have no intention of hurting him," Mark said. "He means a lot to me. Him *and* Peter."

"I heard you were there at Peter's whelping."

"I gave Reese what he asked of me. It was the most precious experience of my life."

"A tad unconventional for an Alpha to attend."

"He refused all other help. I've heard Reese has a stubborn streak."

Carina smirked. "Understatement."

Mark locked his gaze on her. "I have the best of intentions toward him."

"Tell me about those," Carina replied.

Mark looked at me and smiled. "I want to be there for him, to encourage him to smile. I want to protect him and his pup. We've gone from friendship to something more. Quickly but I think we both are feeling a profound connection deep inside. A soul-level connection."

Tears rimmed my eyes and I nodded at him. I felt it too. Every day I felt it.

This amazing wolf had turned my world around.

"You're falling in love with him," Carina said.

I stared at Mark. He looked down at his empty plate. It couldn't be.

"I don't want to scare him off," Mark replied.

"That doesn't answer my question. Do you know or don't you?"

Mark lifted his head and caught my gaze. The lines around his eyes wrinkled with anxiety. He cleared his throat. "I'm headed in that direction."

My face and fingers went numb. I needed to get out. I shoved Carina until she stood and let me past her. I ran for the restroom, slammed a cubicle door closed, and sat on the toilet.

Peter started mewling.

He could sense I was upset. Too fast. Too fast. My heart still belonged to my fated mate. The thought of another wolf loving me made me uneasy. Then why had I even entertained an intimate relationship with Mark? If I wasn't ready, I shouldn't have encouraged him.

I'd asked him to suck my cock this morning.

I scrubbed my hand through my hair.

When I was around Mark, I felt amazing. Hopeful. Warm. I'd been basking in the attention from him. Everything about him felt right. I was so confused; I didn't know what to do.

"Reese?" I recognized Mark's voice and his boots. "I'm sorry. I should have told you first. That was not the way you should have found out how I feel about you."

Maybe that's what it was. Maybe his admission had caught me off guard.

"Reese, I don't want to lose you in my life. If you want me to back off, I will."

That's not what I wanted. I wanted more embraces and intimate moments—not less. I thought about my late mate and my stomach churned. It was guilt I was feeling. I was thinking about moving on without him. But isn't that what he would have wanted?

"Reese, please talk to me."

Tears spilled down my cheeks as I petted little Peter's head. I craved the tenderness Mark had shown me when I was whelping my pup. I craved it from *him*—not just anyone. Having him hold me as I slept last night had filled my dreams with possibilities for us.

Then why was I wanting to run?

I unlatched and opened the door. Mark was leaning against the support posts to either side with both hands. His beautiful brown eyes were glassy.

"I don't want to lose you," he said again. "Please tell me I haven't lost you."

I rose to my feet, sniffed, walked forward, and pressed my forehead to his. "Hold me."

Mark gathered me into his arms, being mindful of little Peter. His hot breath puffed past my ear. "Tell me what you want from me. I'll do whatever you need even if it means walking away."

I buried my face against his neck and inhaled his comforting scent.

"Oh … Mark."

I sobbed as I took a small step away from my late mate and buried myself in Mark's arms. I didn't want him to walk away. What I needed from Mark was his growing affection.

He held me as I cried. As I admitted to myself that my feelings for Mark were taking root in my heart. I was going to be brave and let my relationship with Mark unfold.

"You haven't lost me," I said. "But you need to take me home."

"Right away."

As we left the restroom, Carina ran up to my side.

"Reese, hun, I am *so* sorry," she said. "I shouldn't have pushed so hard. I'm so worried about you getting hurt that I dug too much." She touched Mark's arm. "Mark, I'm sorry. If you're making Reese happy, that's all I've ever wanted for him. I hope I didn't ruin things."

I shook my head. "No, we're good. We have more we need to talk about, that's all."

"I've paid your bill," Carina said. She gave Mark an affectionate shove. "Go. Get him home. Talk. That pup probably needs to feed again."

I zipped up my coat as we stepped out into the cold air. There was supposed to be an arctic wind descending on us tonight. The temperature would plummet. Carina meant well. She always meant well. Being an Alpha made her a bit aggressive. I knew she loved me.

Once home, we rushed into the house and Mark started a fire. I needed to warm up and decompress. At Mark's urging, I shifted and took my place in front of the fireplace.

Peter was greedy, going from teat to teat, rolling and dragging his little body around. He was soon asleep. I nudged him with my nose to make sure he was clean, then let him sleep.

I sighed and dropped my head on the floor, soaking in the warmth. The wind was picking up outside. Mark was reading a book he'd found on my bedside this morning.

I let my wolf brain take over and relaxed. When I woke, my house was dark except for the firelight. The wind was whistling violently past the windows.

"Power is out," Mark said. "I brought in enough wood to last us through the night."

I groaned and rolled onto my elbows. I scanned the carpet. I couldn't see Peter. My heart rate escalated, panicked, and thrummed in my ears. I whined and whimpered.

Peter answered.

Mark had him. Peter was nestled on Mark's lap as he read. He was enjoying the soft stroke of Mark's fingers. My pup smacked his lips and released a toe-curling yawn.

Mark jumped and so did I when Peter let out a sharp bark. His first bark.

And Mark had been there to share it with me. I shifted, grabbed a blanket, and curled up on the sofa beside him. I shuffled down and put my head on his shoulder.

"I meant what I said," Mark said. "About heading there with you."

I pulled the blanket tight around my bare shoulders. "You're sure."

"I've never been surer about anything."

He needed to hear it. He must be beyond worried not knowing how I felt about him. Wondering if he was headed down this road alone. I grasped his arm and kissed his shoulder.

"Me either. I'm right there with you. I want to be with you."

Mark's exhalation came out loud and fast. "I was honestly terrified. I've never felt this way about anyone before. You've made my heart take on all sorts of new shapes. Waking up together this morning and sharing what we did slid so many puzzle pieces in place for me. You've made me examine my life from a different angle. I feel like you were sent to me to complete me."

"Maybe I was."

Mark laughed. "Stubborn and arrogant."

I tugged at his shirt sleeve with my teeth and smiled. We were back on track. Peter stirred and almost flung himself off Mark's lap. His ability to move around was improving. I scratched his head to calm him, and one eye opened slightly. Just a sliver. But enough to see the emerald green that lay beyond his lid. I shook Mark. "He opened an eye!"

"Where?" Mark lifted Peter and held him almost nose to nose with him. "Both eyes."

"What?" I turned Peter to face me. Peering at me. One green eye—one pale blue.

He'd taken something from both of us. Peter and me. I kissed his little nose.

"You're perfect," I said to my pup.

"So are you," Mark said.

Heat flushed my face. Peter had always showered me with romantic talk. It was nice to have that again. Nice to know someone felt that way about me. Nice to know it was Mark.

"You're making me blush," I replied.

"It's the truth. I like everything about you. Your personality, your love for your pup, your eyes … your body. I want all of it in my life."

"I want you in my life too, Mark. I've never met anyone so kind, warm, and sweet."

"It's all the sugar in my coffee."

I full-on laughed. I hadn't done that in a long time. Not since the night before Peter died. We had been in bed, and he was telling me the most ridiculous story. A story he had made up about plumbers, spiders, and annoying customers. He was always doing that—telling me stories.

I went from elation to sadness. Mark set Peter back in his lap.

"Did he pop in on you, Peter's sire?"

"Briefly. Enough to bring me down." I moved away from Mark. "Are you sure you want to do this with me? I'm still an emotional wreck."

"Like we said. We'll take it one day at a time. If you need me to back off, I will. I don't want anything to ruin any relationship we might have. Even if it's just friends."

I shook my head. "No, that would hurt too much. I'd still long for you something fierce."

Peter whined and squirmed. It was time to feed him again. I tossed the blanket aside and took him from Mark. My pup was quick to latch on. The other nipple itched and leaked.

"Please touch it," I said to Mark and looked down at it. There was a perfect bead of milk poised at the tip. Mark reached across me and fingered my soft aching flesh.

It wasn't enough.

"Pinch it."

Mark jerked his head up to look at me. "I don't want to hurt you."

"Little Peter is doing much worse to me, trust me."

Mark applied pressure with his finger and thumb. My lower gut churned, and my cock throbbed. He pinched harder. I threw my head back and moaned as I shifted in my seat.

He released my nipple. The top side of his hand was covered in milk. He took it to his lips and cleaned it off with his tongue. Keeping Peter latched on, I leaned toward Mark and invited him to kiss me by whispering his name and telling him how much I wanted him.

It had the desired effect. He raked his hands into my hair and brought my mouth to his. Little Peter released my nipple, sighed, and made the noises that meant he was going back to sleep.

I tipped away from Mark, rose from the sofa, and placed Peter in his pup bed by the fire. Mark's gaze wandered over my naked body as I returned to the sofa.

I sank to my knees between his legs.

I brushed my hand up and down his thigh. His cock had swollen behind his fly. I placed my hand on it, caressing the bulk, then hovered over it, and placed my mouth on his hardening girth.

I used my lips, tongue, and teeth to tease him until he was undulating beneath my mouth and grasping handfuls of my hair. I wanted more. I unlatched his button and lowered his fly. He shifted so I could retrieve his cock from its confines. I lowered his underwear and took in the sight of his thick glistening cockhead. As with everything else, it had been a long time since I'd been on my knees like this. It felt right. I felt no guilt. Mark meant something to me.

I licked his slit and ran my tongue around the rim of his head. He groaned and cupped my face in his gentle hand, his fingers around the back of my neck, his thumb across my ear.

His touch made me feel like I was precious to him.

I knew I was.

I sucked on his cockhead then applied more suction as I lowered my mouth around him. His velvety smoothness and the taste of virility had me humming as I worked his cock.

I took a moment to lick the underside with the tip of my tongue as I looked at him. Mark's eyes were hooded; his mouth open as he watched me.

He licked his lips.

"Haul off your pants," I said to him. I shuffled back so he had space to remove his pants. He threw them and his underwear to the end of the sofa.

My next instructions. "Sit, shuffle down, and spread your legs."

He did as he was told. His lust was too far gone to deny me anything. I grasped his cock in my hand and pumped it, then sucked his full length back into my mouth.

I let it pop from my lips and licked my finger.

"Do you trust me?"

His pupils blown; Mark nodded his head. He jumped a little as I burrowed my way between his ass cheeks with my finger. I found my target and Mark flinched, then relaxed.

The moan he emitted as I pressed my finger past his tight ring of muscle was as sweet a sound as game being brought to the ground. My cock pulsed. It wanted into that constricting space.

Peter and I had engaged in sexual play that was unconventional by traditional role standards. He had often let me, his Omega, penetrate him, an Alpha.

I had come to enjoy it immensely.

Mark squirmed as I pressed my finger higher into him. I took his cock back into my mouth, bobbing and sucking. I couldn't quite reach his gland, but I'd made an introduction to what I wanted someday. He had to know where I was going with this, and he wasn't objecting.

His breath started to escape rapid fire, panting and groaning. I increased the speed and pressure on his cock, keeping my finger inside him like an erotic plug.

The base of his cock swelled, creating a knot. I licked and sucked it, using my tongue to tease his skin. It was hard and warm beneath my lips. Mark grasped handfuls of my hair.

I gripped his knot in my hand, caressing it, and sucked his cock into my mouth. As I rubbed the swollen base, I slipped his cockhead to the base of my tongue, then sucked it all the way back to my lips. I twirled my tongue around his slit, then swallowed him again.

I felt his knot release.

Mark swore and spilled down my throat. I kept him encased until his body slowed and he twitched each time I ran my tongue over his tip. I slurped and left his softening cock to rest on his wiry greying pubes and removed my finger from his body.

I rose from his groin to his lips which were waiting for me. He wasn't frantic. He just needed to reconnect. We were slow with each other. Simply enjoying the connection.

"We should go to bed," he said after he released me.

I agreed and gathered up Peter. After setting him on the bed, I made a quick trip to the bathroom to wash my hand and brush my teeth. Mark was waiting for me when I entered the bedroom. His pants were still off, and he'd removed his shirt. He pulled back the bedding and climbed in. Mark moved Peter aside for a second so I could get in next to him. Once my back was flush with Mark's chest, I pulled Peter's bed to be at my stomach.

Mark felt *so* good behind me. The abundant hair on his chest tickled my back in a way I found comforting. He'd slung his arm over my waist. His soft cock was at my tailbone. And he'd tossed a leg over my thigh, pulling me to him. Almost possessively.

I felt thoroughly protected which made the Omega part of me content. I knew Mark would make sure nothing bad ever happened to me again. At least, as much as he could control.

I rubbed my stump across the fingers of the hand he had resting at my waist. He took it in his grasp so I could bring his hand up to my lips. I lingered as I rested my lips on his fingers.

If I wasn't still sore from whelping, I would be looking for a deeper physical connection. I knew we would get there, I just needed to be patient.

Mark kissed the back of my neck and snuffled his nose against my hair. I kissed his fingers again. His soft brown eyes had let me in. I was halfway down a path I thought I would never be traveling down again. Tears rimmed my eyes and escaped down my cheek.

I'm sorry, Peter.

You'd like Mark ... I know you would.

I closed my eyes and soaked in the feeling of Mark holding me. I didn't have one single nightmare that night. Mark woke with me each time Peter needed to be fed and kissed my shoulder as I arranged the pup at a nipple to suckle. Then Mark would fall asleep behind me.

In the morning, we caressed a response out of each other's bodies.

It was the perfect way to wake up with him.
Waking up with him was perfect.

Chapter Seven | Mark

I arrived home to find a note on my door. I'd broken my connection with my wolf pack, directing them to only interrupt me if it was urgent. I wanted my entire focus to be on Reese and Peter this past weekend. A weekend that had offered me so much more than I'd been expecting.

I opened the note.

Where have you been? it read.

I rolled my eyes and opened a connection with my lead Beta, Allegra.

Me: "I had some work over in Creekside."

Allegra: "What kind of work? They have a plumbing company."

Me: "More like general construction-type stuff. A renovation gone wrong."

Allegra: "They have wolves there who can do that."

Me: "He preferred to have me work on it."

Allegra: "Why?"

Me: "Because he did."

Allegra: "Is he a wolf?"

Me: "An Omega."

Allegra: "And you stayed overnight. Why?"

Me: "So I could start early."

Allegra: "I'm coming over."

There was no point telling her not to show up at my house. She'd do it anyway. She took her role in the pack seriously. She needed to know everything about everyone.

Even me.

I went inside and waited for her. Put on a pot of coffee in my new machine. It worked better than the old one. Not much, but better. It had just started to brew when the front door opened.

As leader, I had very little privacy.

Allegra sat on a stool at my kitchen island. "Tell me why when there are perfectly good construction companies in Creekside that you needed to spend the last two weekends going there."

"Reese isn't feeling comfortable with asking his pack for anything at the moment?"

"Reese?"

"Yes, that's his name."

"Why isn't he comfortable relying on his pack? Did he do something wrong?"

"No, he's a good and loyal wolf."

"Then why?"

I groaned. "You and your *why* questions."

"That's how I find out things. You *like* it when I find out things."

"Not when it comes to me." She wasn't going to let up. "He lost his mate, and he has a new pup. He doesn't want to be a burden to his pack."

"How much are you charging him?"

"I'm not."

"So … he can be a burden *to you* but not his pack."

"I offered."

"Mark." Allegra crossed her arms. "He's part of a rival pack. I know you've been going over there to visit Hunter but aside from that, we need to stick to our territory. Hunter still feels like family. It's understandable. Helping some random Creekside wolf is not."

"He's not random."

Allegra grunted. "What does that mean?"

"It means we've gotten to know each other." That's all she was squeezing out of me.

"He's a rival."

"He's harmless."

She crossed the kitchen and poured herself a glass of water from the sink. "I'd like to repeat that you didn't come home last night." She stared at me as she leaned against the counter. "Your pack might have needed you. You were almost two hours away."

"Ninety minutes and I didn't want to make the trip. You had things under control."

"Alpha, you have an excuse for everything. This behavior is unlike you. And don't you dare give me any guff about it being hard for you to drive in the dark now."

"That's not why I stayed. There was a vicious storm in Creekside. His power went out. He was all alone in the house with his pup."

Allegra jammed her fists onto her hips. "And Friday night? What's your excuse for that?"

Of course, she knew about that. She lived next door. She probably saw me leave, suspicious after I told her I was going to sever connection with the pack for a few days.

"You had every intention of staying there all weekend," she said. "Why?"

"Are you digging for a conclusion you've already formulated in your head?"

"One that better not be true."

I sighed. "Allegra, leave me alone."

"Okay … appease me. Pick one of the three female wolves in our pack to be your mate."

I stormed across the kitchen and grabbed a coffee cup. "I'm not going to do that."

"Why?"

"For fuck's sake. Stop asking me. I'm not interested in them."

"Because you're interested in someone else."

She'd worn me down. "Yes."

"This male Omega over in Creekside."

I nodded. "Yes."

"I didn't think you liked males."

"I didn't … until I met Reese."

"You want to make him your mate?"

"We're not there yet."

"That can't happen … you know that. He's already had a pup by some other wolf."

I poured some coffee and mixed in my milk and sugar. "I don't care."

"You have to care. That pup's sire was a rival. We won't accept it into our pack."

It was true. Traditionally, I couldn't accept a pup into our pack if it was the result of a rival wolf's mating. Reese would never agree to be separated from his pup. To leave him with his pack so he could become my mate and follow me to my home … to my pack.

His love was too fierce for little Peter.

I could go against the pack and bring Peter to my home but then Reese would be ostracized by my pack members. He'd be made to feel unwelcome. He might eventually leave me.

"I need you to go," I said.

"End this," Allegra said as she headed for the door. "Right now, before you get in too deep."

"I'll take your suggestion under advisement."

Allegra bowed to me. "Alpha."

I pressed the door closed and stood there with my hand on it. I hadn't considered the implications of starting a relationship with Reese. That we might someday fall in love and want to live together. And what that would look like. It hadn't even crossed my mind; I was so wrapped up in the affection of the young wolf.

The week dragged by. The only bright spot was each night when Reese phoned me. The plan was, I'd be heading out on Friday night to spend the night with him. I'd put off bringing up what Allegra had reminded me about, that Peter wouldn't be welcome in our pack.

It was Thursday night. I couldn't put it off any longer. We needed to figure out if we were going to continue moving forward. Moving toward a future together.

I picked up the ringing phone. "Hey, you."

"Hey."

"Did you have a good day?"

"It was. It was a good day. Peter is growing fast, moving around really well on his own. His eyes are completely open now. I love looking into them and imagining what he's thinking."

"He's thinking that his carrier loves him."

"I hate that word—carrier."

"What would you rather be called?"

"I like the human word, *Papa*."

"Then he knows how much his Papa loves him." I would never ask Reese to consider being separated from his pup. Our only option would be Reese living in a pack that shunned him.

I couldn't ask him to do that either.

"Reese, I need to talk about something."

"That sounds serious. Can it wait until you come out tomorrow night?"

"I might not be coming."

Dead silence on the other end of the line.

"Reese?"

"You're backing out?"

"My Beta brought a few things to my attention."

"Of course, they did."

"What happens if we decide to become mates? My pack won't accept Peter because he was sired by a rival. And they would shun you if I went against them and brought you both home."

"I'm not giving Peter up for my pack to raise."

"No, of course not. I don't want you to."

"Then where does that leave us?"

"I don't know."

"What does your heart tell you?"

"That I want to be with you more than my next breath."

"Me too. Please come to see me tomorrow night."

I couldn't deny him. I just couldn't. My heart was being pulled hard toward him. If this was the end, I wanted one last weekend with him. To soak him up and memorize everything.

"I'll be there."

"I'm safeguarding a mind-blowing kiss for you."

I smiled. "Me too, Reese. Me too."

THE DRIVE SEEMED LONGER than usual, I wanted to get to Reese so badly. I'd received an earful from Allegra when I'd asked her to mind the pack for me again.

I'd told her I was *handling* things.

Truth was, I had no idea what I was doing. All I knew is I needed to hold Reese again. To feel his bare skin against me. To inhale the addicting scent of him.

And of little Peter.

It was easier with Peter. He was innocent and uncomplicated. I'd loved him since the moment he was born. The fact Reese's body had produced him made him even more loveable.

And why is that, Mark?

My heart ached. I had set out with the intention of winding things down with Reese. The thought of following through made me feel nauseous. It's not what I wanted.

Our situation was impossible.

Reese was shivering on his front porch when I arrived. His brow was dipped, his eyes sorrowful. He knew why I was there. We would have one last weekend together.

I launched myself up the steps and into his arms. I gathered him up and found his lips. I didn't care who saw us. Everyone already knew we were together.

And they'd welcomed me.

Lucas' pack had welcomed me.

Reese's happiness overrode any rivalry we had between our two packs. They'd been presented with couplings over the years that tested their traditions. They'd adapted.

Unlike my pack. They were strict and unforgiving. I had no room to live my life the way I wanted even though I was their pack leader.

Reese hauled me into the house and continued his assault on my lips in the front entry. He was frantic to unzip and pull off my coat. I dropped my coat to the floor and toed off my boots.

"We only have a few minutes. Peter has just fallen asleep."

I followed Reese to the living room. On the coffee table, a bottle of wine and two glasses. In front of the roaring fire on the floor, a bear fur. My cock thickened as my imagination created images of what Reese had planned for us tonight.

"Take off your clothes," he said. "Quick."

I smiled as I obeyed and watched Reese strip. It was almost comical. As if we were trying to rut before Reese's sire came home. The only one interrupting us would be Peter.

He was tucked safely in his pup bed in reach of the fire's warmth.

Reese stretched out on the fur and invited me into his arms. I descended on his mouth as my chest made contact with his, our hardening cocks pressed between us.

He was ravenous. So was I. The mind-blowing kiss he had promised me came at me full force. His lips—his tongue. Even his teeth. He wrapped his legs around my waist and undulated his hips, rocking his hard cock to caress mine. He held my face and looked up into my eyes.

"I want you, Mark," he said. "I want to feel you moving inside me."

My cock pulsed. My body had never wanted something as much as the wolf beneath me.

"I want you too. Are you healed enough?"

Reese smiled up at me. "I'm all good."

I closed my mouth over his and moaned as he used his heels to pull me closer to him. He raked the fingers of one hand through my hair. "Mate with me," he whispered.

Tears collected in my eyes. It was true. What we'd shared had never been rutting. What we'd shared had always been leading to fully mating. I guided my cock, adjusting to the difference in his body from any female I had ever rutted with. I traced his hole with my cockhead.

Reese was warm and wet. I was gentle as I caressed my cock inside him. He gasped and threw his head back, his chin jutting into the air. I leaned forward and set my teeth to it.

He groaned and clutched my ass in his hand, his stump on my other ass cheek, encouraging me to sink further into him. I adjusted my position and pressed forward. My cock was enveloped by the softest, snuggest space, that tightened around my shaft, drawing me in.

I nearly spilled my seed.

I took a deep breath and closed the space between us. Reese's hand moved from my ass to my face. He stroked my cheek as I withdrew and thrust with care.

"Yes." Reese kept his gaze on mine. "More."

I repeated my undulation, trying to judge from Reese's eyes if I was hurting him. He parted his lips and mewled as I repeated my motion, faster this time.

"Yeah," Reese hissed. "That's it. Mate with me."

Those words did something to my insides—and to my cock. I took his mouth and pumped harder. His moans filled my throat. His hand clutched the back of my neck.

Panting, I pulled away. We didn't take our eyes off each other. The faster I thrust, the more blown his pupils became. A truth bubbled up inside me as I mated with him.

Reese groaned, rhythmic with each thrust, his chest heaving, thick eyelashes fluttering.

Tears streamed from Reese's eyes to his cheeks.

"Mark," he whispered as he looked back and forth between both my eyes. More tears and he gripped my face. "Mark—I," he mewled.

I cupped his face in my hands. "I know … I feel it too."

I slowed my hips.

"I'm yours," I said, starting the ceremony.

"And I'm yours," Reese replied.

I thrust high into him and layered my body on his. I kept rocking my hips as I licked the area of his skin between his neck and his shoulder. The scent and taste brought out my inner wolf. He was mine. He wanted to be mine. And I was his. Hell with the world.

I opened my mouth as my canines descended—and sunk them into Reese's flesh. His blood flooded my mouth. His consciousness shimmered at the periphery of my mind.

Reese growled and used his strong arms to roll me onto my back. He sat astride me, rising and falling, his head back, his cock bouncing seductively.

In one swift motion, he shot forward, his hair brushing my cheek, and bit down on my claiming area. He clung to my flesh until our mind connection was complete.

Reese: "I love you."

My heart felt like it was percolating inside my chest, my emotions raw and wired. There was only one thing to say. Reese completed me.

Me: "I love you too."

Reese released me, curved his chest away from me, sitting high again, and opened his throat, a howl as beautiful and full of emotion as I'd ever heard.

I joined him in a song of mating and love as he continued to ride my cock, his hand on my thigh, his stump on my belly to balance himself.

I grasped his thighs, bucking into him. Every thrust bringing me closer. Reese bounced harder and faster. His cock bobbed in front of me. I took it into my palm and stroked him.

He looked gorgeous, riding my cock, blood running down his chest. His puffy nipples releasing streams of milk along his ribcage.

Reese licked his lips—and groaned.

His seed spurted onto my chest, as heated as his eyes as he looked down at me.

My belly quivered, my lust at its peak. Wrapping my hands around Reese's waist, the depths behind my groin ached and my balls lifted.

"Reese," I moaned as my ass clenched and I filled my beautiful, loving mate with enough seed to flood him. Enough to one day put another pup in him.

That's what I wanted.

I ran my hand up his chest, mixing the blood and milk, and circled his weeping nipple with the smeared mess. He placed his hand to the left of my head, leaned forward, and kissed me.

A joining of two souls. That's what we'd done.

His lips spoke the truth of it.

We were destined to be together. We might not be fated, but we had found each other. And now there was no parting us. We'd claimed each other. For now, that was enough.

Come Monday, my pack would be wanting answers for my absence.

I wasn't sure what to tell them.

Chapter Eight | Reese

I knocked on Jonas and Damon's door and waited while checking on Peter. He was happily squirming and looking up into my eyes as he tried to dig out of the blankets I had wrapped him in against the cold. He was squawking and squeaking and beyond precious.

Mark and I had laid in bed this morning just watching him sleep.

Mark had whispered," I love you," to him after kissing his head.

I had started crying. Our love was complete. Mark loved me and my pup. My late mate couldn't have asked for anything more than that. A wolf to love us both.

I exhaled a long breath as Damon opened the door.

I pasted on a smile. My business here was serious. I needed advice.

"Hi, Reese," Damon said and peered into the folds of the blankets. I was wearing the snuggie again. It was a lifesaver. I could always keep Peter with me. "Aw, he's so cute."

Damon looked past me. "No Mark?"

"Mark is at my house tiling the backsplash in the kitchen this morning. Thought it best if we talked as a pack before involving him."

"Probably for the best," Lucas said from behind Damon. Normally, we wouldn't have met in person, but Damon wasn't able to access the pack's link. His opinion was valued by the pack.

I entered the family room. Those included in today's conversation. Lucas and Adam, and Jonas and Damon. Bryant, Grayson, and Hunter. Carina and her new mate, Kal.

And my brother, Harlan.

He looked annoyed, arms crossed, glaring at me.

I took a seat on the sofa.

"According to the howling last night," Lucas said, "you claimed each other."

I cleared my throat. "We did."

"Moment of passion?" Jonas asked. "Damon and I have been there."

"No." Hunter spoke up. "Their song spoke of love."

Harlan grunted.

I wiped my palm on my pant leg. Last night should have had my pack *fully* rejoicing. They *were* thrilled for me, but they were also worried. They didn't know much about Mark's pack.

I wasn't sure what their reaction was going to be when I told them. The Riverton pack was different from ours. More traditional. My pack wouldn't like what I was going to tell them.

"Tell us what we need to know," Lucas said. "You said there was a problem."

I chew on my bottom lip as I phrased my wording.

"Riverton is strict," I said. "They follow the old ways."

Harlan leaned forward. "Meaning what?"

"It means they won't accept Peter into the pack."

Damon bolted to his feet. "What?"

Jonas frowned. "You're not thinking of giving Peter up, are you?"

I shook my head. "Never. Not even for Mark."

"Then what is going to happen?" Carina asked. "His pack won't keep letting him visit every weekend. There will be a revolt. He'll be challenged, injured, or even killed."

"My mate is strong," I replied.

"He's in his 50s, Reese," Adam said.

Adam was right. To keep seeing each other the way we'd had would put Mark at risk. He needed to stay with his pack. They wouldn't challenge him if I moved to Riverton with him.

We were mates. We'd claimed each other. We should be living together.

But my pup came first.

I played with the top of Peter's head. He needed to be part of a pack. I loved Mark but I wouldn't sacrifice the happiness and wellbeing of my pup.

I lowered my hand from Peter's head and stared at his little nose. I'd found love again and I couldn't stay with him. I'd found a chosen mate my heart ached for, but it couldn't be.

Carina rubbed my back as tears rolled down my cheeks.

"I can't be with him, can I?"

"I'm sorry, Reese," Adam said. "Not unless you leave Peter with us."

"I won't do that."

"I knew he was a bad idea," Harlan said. "I told you, Reese, I didn't like it."

Adam walked over to Harlan and placed his hand on Harlan's shoulder. "This is not the time for that. Your brother is going to need our support."

I rose from the sofa. "I need to go home. I need to be with Mark."

Carina launched onto her feet and hugged me. "I'm so sorry, hun."

Lucas wandered over. "Go. Be with him. Spend your last night together."

The walk back was solemn. Mark knew why I had gone over there. He had to have known what the consensus would be. He was sitting on the floor near the fireplace when I arrived.

He was down on his knees, ass to heels, staring into the firelight.

"It's over, isn't it," he said.

I took my time getting to him, not wanting to answer his question. Once there, I stood behind him and put my hand on his shoulder. "I love you, Mark, but Peter comes first. He needs a pack."

"I only want what's best for him. I love him too."

I kneeled beside him. "I know you do. It breaks my heart that he won't know you."

Mark turned to me; his face coated in tears. "I love you so much."

I stroked his face, dispensing with some of the tears, then combed his temple with my fingertips. "I never knew my heart would love like this again."

He shook his head. "I'll never mate with another."

That saddened me, deeply. I wanted Mark to be happy. I wanted his life to be filled with good days. A mate and pups might bring him that happiness.

I joined him, unable to control my tears. "Don't say that."

Mark shuffled to face me. "There will only be you. You have become my world." He pressed his forehead to mine. "You're my Reese … my forever love."

I went from crying to sobbing, sucking raspy breaths in and out. This couldn't be happening. The universe had played a third cruel trick on me.

"I need you to mate with me," I said. I needed to feel him inside me, caressing me.

Loving me.

Mark lifted Peter from the snuggie on my chest, set him on the floor, and helped me out of the contraption. Once I was free, he unbuttoned my flannel shirt. He stripped it off my shoulders and arms and tossed it to one side. He captured my mouth in the tenderest of kisses.

I was going to remember every move he made. Every taste. Every feeling. Every scent and sight. His mouth tasted of coffee, cream, and sugar. His lips were warm and wet. He held me like he'd never get to again. Tears streaked down my cheeks. His scent was clean and familiar.

He moved away, lifted Peter, and nodded toward the hallway.

"Let's spend what time we have left in the bedroom."

We walked hand in hand with Mark carrying Peter. He set my pup on the bed. I looked at Peter. In a way, he was *our* pup. Not just Peter's sire and me, but Mark's and mine.

He'd been there from the start of Peter's life.

He loved Peter as his own.

I shimmied my pants onto the floor and climbed onto the bed. Mark positioned Peter on a nipple and waited for him to suckle. Our pup needed to take from both sides now.

Mark sat on the bed and petted the fur along his back.

When Peter was done with one side, I rolled over and he latched onto my other nipple. I could hear rustling behind me. The bed dipped and Mark lay down, his hot bare flesh heating my back. He kissed me from my shoulder up to my neck, stopping to lick where he had bit me.

"I'm yours," he whispered.

My tears ran and dripped off my nose.

"I'll always be yours," I replied.

I looked down at our sleeping pup, milk dribbling out of his mouth. He was full and done. I was on my left side. I couldn't move him without getting up.

"Can you put Peter in the pup bed?" I asked Mark.

Mark reached his arm over me and put Peter in his bed. He traced his fingers along my arm on the way back, starting at my stump and ending at my shoulder. Then down my ribs, waist, and hip to my thigh. He moved over and gently rolled me onto my back.

I gasped; his lips were so soft as they kissed my belly. My senses were like static, tingling as his mouth moved over my body. He started at my feet, showing me his devotion with small kisses and licks as he moved up my ankles, to my shins, to my thighs, to my hips—stomach to chest to shoulders, and up my throat to my lips. He used tender hands to separate my thighs.

I gripped his shoulder as he caressed his cock into me.

He thrust and retreated, rocking slowly, as he gazed down at me. His lips parted and he hauled in a ragged breath as tears fell from his sorrowful brown eyes.

This was going to crush us both.

He stopped his hips and buried his face alongside my neck, behind my ear, breathing heavily. "I can't leave you," he whispered. "I just can't."

"Mark … I can't go with you. Peter's life is too precious."

He lifted his head, let out a howl of anguish, and thrust into me, tears spilling down his face. Three thrusts in and he stopped and collapsed on me.

I wrapped my arms around him and inhaled the scent of his neck.

"I love you," I said.

"I'm leaving," he whispered.

"Already?" I clutched him to me. "I thought we had until morning. Please don't go yet."

"I'm never leaving your side … ever again."

I pushed on him until he was looking down at me.

"You're not making any sense," I said.

"The pack. Riverton. I'm leaving. I'm never going back there again."

My heart thundered. A leader didn't leave his pack. Not for any reason other than death or defeat. Or the passing of the leadership to their heir.

"Mark, you can't. They're your pack."

Mark locked his gaze on mine. "You're my pack. You and Peter."

I shuddered and pulled him into my arms. I sobbed against his cheek, overwhelmed with joy *and* sadness by what Mark was willing to give up for me.

To be with me.

To be with me and Peter.

I howled loud and clear. My mate had chosen me.

He'd chosen me and our love.

Outside, the sound of my pack celebrating with me. With us. We didn't need to be our own pack. Mark was part of East Creekside now.

Chapter Nine | Mark

It wasn't as easy as simply never going back. After Reese and I mated a few times last night, we'd taken a moment to discuss the details of what I'd promised him.

I meant it.

I was leaving Riverton.

My life was with Reese. And Reese was in Creekside.

I needed to phone my brother, Declan. He deserved the right to claim leadership of the Riverton pack. Maybe city life wasn't agreeing with him. Maybe he craved the wilderness.

If he was interested, he'd need to be there when I told my pack I was stepping down.

I reclined on Reese's sofa and listened to ring after ring.

"Hello."

Gruff. He hadn't recognized the number. Declan had one of those fancy cell phones that told you which one of your contacts was calling.

"It's me."

"Mark. What's up?"

"I met someone."

"Fated mate?"

"No. Chosen. It's serious."

"How serious?"

"We're mated."

"Claimed and mated."

"Yes. His name is Reese."

"You don't like males."

"I love this one."

"Claimed, mated, and loved."

"He makes me whole."

"Congratulations, big brother. Anything else?"

"I'm stepping down … from Riverton."

Silence.

"Declan?"

"I'm surprised. It's all you ever wanted."

"I found something much more precious."

"I don't understand. Why give up the leadership?"

"Reese is from Creekside."

"So, take him home with you."

"He has a pup … from a mating with a rival."

"He's been mated before?"

"His mate died."

"And the pack won't accept the pup."

"And they'd shun Reese."

Declan sighed. "What do you want from me, brother?"

"To offer you the leadership."

Declan laughed hard and sharp. "You're joking, right?"

"It's what our sire would want."

"It's not what *I* want."

It had been a long shot. Declan was obviously happy with what he was doing in the city. Now, I'd be subjected to the tradition of succession. I couldn't just leave the pack.

I had to be chased out.

I'd need to shift and take on a challenger—and put up a proper fight.

"I'm telling the pack tomorrow, Sunday at dusk."

"I won't be there." The background noise became muffled. He was speaking to someone. He came back on the line. "I need to go back to work. Best of luck, Mark."

"Yeah … you too."

Reese clung to my arm as I hung up. "Well?"

"He doesn't want to do it."

"But that means you have to fight."

"If I want to keep any kind of honor. I would never disrespect my sire by disgracing our family. He handed the leadership to me. He trusted me with it."

"I don't like the idea of you fighting a much younger wolf."

"I'll hold my own. Let him get a few good strikes in and then run."

Reese brushed his hand along my jawline. "I want to be there."

I frowned. "You'll be amongst rivals. They won't be kind."

"I want to be there for you. Let them know I'm not afraid of them."

"You'll need to leave Peter with someone."

"Adam has one of those chest pumps. I'll pump before we go, and Adam can watch Peter. He has more than enough experience with young pups."

I inhaled a long breath and exhaled with concession. Reese wouldn't back down. His stubbornness would win out. I didn't stand a chance of winning this one.

"We should go to bed," I said.

Reese smiled. "Any plans once we get there?"

I smirked. "You know I do. I'm going to mate you into the mattress."

Reese laughed. "Dirty talk. I love it."

I laughed along with him. "Just stating facts, Omega."

Reese leaped to his feet. "Yes, sir, Alpha."

I lifted Peter in his pup bed and chased Reese down the hallway. He squealed the whole way to the bedroom as he kept just ahead of me. The noise woke up Peter.

Reese would have to feed him back to sleep.

I didn't mind. I loved watching Peter feed. Another 3 weeks and we'd wean him off chest milk and start him on a meat pablum. He'd still feed for comfort, but it wouldn't be as often.

Our sleep was broken by Peter's hunger and our need to mate. I filled Reese with seed again and again. We had to shuffle our sleeping arrangement over, the sheets were so damp.

The sunlight broke on a day that would change the course of my life forever. I'd made a commitment to Reese as his mate. I had no intention of backing down on that.

I looked at myself in the mirror of the ensuite. My body had predictably aged since the last time I had been challenged for the leadership. I'd sent them away whimpering and running.

That wasn't my intention this time.

This time, I was going to lose.

There was every chance I'd end up with some serious injuries. Reese knew that even though he didn't understand it. Lucas was appalled they would put me through the ritual.

I'd been the Riverton leader for over twenty-five years.

Lucas thought that deserved some respect.

Being part of the Creekside pack was going to be different. Not being the leader was going to be difficult, but I was willing to endure the discomfort for Reese and Peter's sake.

They were my family now.

I flexed my muscles. All my years of running and plumbing had kept me fit.

Reese snuck into the bathroom and ran his fingers through the hair on my chest. "You're perfection, my mate. He kissed my shoulder. "What's on the agenda today?"

"I need to distract myself. I'm going to tackle that linoleum in the bedrooms. I brought the materials in last night to warm them up."

"What time are we leaving?"

"I'd like to leave at 2:00. I have some things to do around my house before I make my announcement. The new leader will take over the house. I'll need to be packed."

"You won't get a chance to move out properly? What about all your stuff?"

"I've tried not to collect much. I'll have to leave behind what I do have."

Reese frowned. "It's barbaric, the whole business."

"It's the old ways. I don't belong to a democracy like East Creekside."

"Then you should have more authority to stop this challenge."

"That decision is out of my hands. It's tradition."

Reese made a funny noise with his lips and left me to contemplate my evening. I knew who would be challenging me. A 32-year-old Alpha male who had mated last year, Colin. He often disagreed with my decisions. It had angered him that I risked my life when I rescued Hunter's family. And that I took Hunter's sire to East Creekside every few weeks to visit.

I looked down at the sink. Now, there would be no one to drive his sire to Hunter's.

I hated to let him down, but once I was chased off the territory, I wouldn't be allowed to return—for any reason. Even to help an elderly wolf visit his offspring's family.

Plus, Allegra would probably lose her position in the pack. The new leadership had an Omega. A lot of what Allegra did for me fell into the roles of an Omega mated to the leader.

This change in leadership affected more than just me.

I pictured Reese's broody face. He was my mate. I loved him. I would give up my entire world to be with him. And that's what I was doing. Giving it all up for my chosen mate.

I pulled on a shirt and headed for the first of the bedrooms I was going to be working on today. Thankfully, Peter's sire had already cut the linoleum to size. I just needed to glue it down.

By the time 1:40 rolled around, I had both bedrooms done. The rooms just needed to have the trim reattached. I could do that tomorrow if I felt up to it. I'd be living here now.

I wanted everything perfect for Reese and Peter.

I'd received so many thank you's for installing that dishwasher that I'd had to tell Reese to cool it. Instead, now, I received a kiss every time he filled or emptied it.

That was fine by me.

I dressed in clothes that were easy to take off and on. Reese would hold onto them for me. Meet me on the road with the truck to pick me up, my belongings in the box.

It was silent in the cab as we drove to Riverton. When I pulled up to my house, no one was around. Thankfully. Reese was with me. I didn't want to explain his existence yet.

Allegra hadn't spread news of him through our pack's network.

She'd afforded me that much respect for my privacy.

We headed for my bedroom first. I hauled three suitcases out of my closet that had been left there by a previous leader. Reese helped me pick out what I should bring and I folded it and packed as much as I could into two of the suitcases. The third would be for personal items.

Reese perused the living room.

"What are you going to bring?" he asked as he lifted a frame with a photo of my sire. "Pictures, for sure. Do you have any other memorabilia?"

"I don't want to clutter up your place."

"*Our* place. It's your home now too."

I smiled. "I don't want to fill *our* home with junk." I headed for the fireplace area. To the right of the fireplace was a quilt rack with an assortment of quilts my carrier had sewn. I retrieved three of those and crammed them into the suitcase. There was enough spare space for the pictures.

I looked around the room. I'd spent my entire life in this house. I wandered into the kitchen, remembering all the meals we'd had there together as a family. All the good times.

Reese wrapped his arms around my waist from behind and set his chin on my shoulder. "You're giving up a lot for me. Are you sure this is what you want?"

I turned to him and held his face.

"You're my life now. My love for you is endless and overshadows every one of my life experiences of my past. You are the reason I draw breath. You and Peter."

Reese clung to me and buried his face against my shoulder.

"I love you so much."

I was about to speak but a scent caught my attention and then my front door opened.

Allegra.

"Who's this?" she asked as she entered the kitchen.

"This is Reese. The Omega I told you about."

Allegra sneered as she looked Reese up and down.

"He's disabled."

"I assure you, he is not."

"Where's his pup?"

"Safely at home," Reese replied.

Allegra looked at me. "You're moving him here?"

I shook my head. "No."

Allegra looked back toward the front entry where all of my luggage was crowding the door. She had assumed they belonged to someone else.

"Whose bags are those?" she asked.

"Mine," I answered.

There was a moment of surprise when her eyebrows rose, and she scowled at me. "Surely, you're not planning on leaving your pack for this disabled Omega."

"Reese. He's not disabled. And yes, I am."

Allegra snorted. "I always knew you were soft, but this is beyond deranged even."

"I'm making the announcement at dusk."

"You'll have to fight a challenger."

"I'm well aware."

"It'll be Colin. You'll receive some real damage."

Reese clung to my arm. "My mate is prepared to take him on."

Allegra's eyes opened wide. "Your mate?"

"We claimed each other," I said.

"Mark …. " She took a step toward us. "Why? We have three females for you to choose from."

"Seems I'm not interested in females after all. Reese helped me discover that."

"But mated to him? Surely, he's not worth giving up your leadership for."

"He's more than worth it." I put my arm around Reese and tugged him to me. I kissed the side of his head. "I love him. And I love his little pup."

"*Our* pup."

I turned Reese in my arms to look at him. Tears rimmed my eyes. I knew I was going to become Peter's sire. But I'd never thought Reese would consider his as mine.

"What?" I whispered.

"He'll always be Peter's and mine … but you love him like your own. You were there when he was whelped. You've told me you loved him from that moment. You have been attentive, gentle, and loving toward him. I consider him to be *ours*."

"Hate to break this up," Allegra said. "But it's dusk."

"I'll always treat him as my own." I kissed Reese, ignoring the snorting noise coming from Allegra. I would make my announcement over our joined connection.

I hung on to Reese's hand.

Me: "I have an announcement." I burst through everyone's privacy screen.

There were a flurry of minds coming to attention.

Colin: "Anything to do with that Omega I detected with you?"

Me: "Yes, everything to do with him. He's my mate."

Colin: "He's not from here."

Me: "He's from East Creekside. And that's where I'm going. I'm stepping down."

The noise was deafening as everyone started asking questions. Questions turned to outrage as I told them how I'd met my mate and fallen in love with him and his pup.

Colin: "I challenge you."

Me: "And you'll make a good leader." Colin was on the aggressive side, but he was also fair in his assessment of things. We had disagreed over the years, but he had never presented an argument that he hadn't thought through. He always had the welfare of the pack on his mind.

Colin: "Meet me out front of your house."

Me: "Give me a second to load up my things."

Colin projected his consent through the link. I took a deep breath as I thought through what I needed to do. Load up my luggage was the first thing. Then put Reese in the truck with my clothes. He'd be safer there and he'd still be able to see what was going on.

"Reese, can you give me a hand with my stuff?"

He smirked at me. It was a running joke. *Only one hand to give.* He hauled the suitcase containing the quilts outside and slung it into the back of my truck.

I loaded up the other two. My life in three suitcases.

"I need you to stay in the truck," I said to Reese. "And keep the doors locked. Be ready to take off down the driveway as soon as I'm run off."

"Why?"

"Some of my pack is seeing red when it comes to you. They've been loyal to me throughout the years. They don't believe you're worthy of me. They want to challenge you."

Reese wrinkled his brow. "I can't fight."

"They know that. Allegra told them about your missing hand." I opened the driver's side truck door. "That's why you need to stay in the truck." I looked over my shoulder.

Everyone was arriving.

"Quick, get in."

Reese climbed in, locked the doors, and rolled down the window. I removed my clothes and handed them through to Reese. Everything tossed onto the bench seating, he reached for me.

"I love you," he said.

"I love you too." I leaned through the window and kissed him. A chorus of growls chastised my show of affection. I didn't care. I kissed him again.

"Close the window."

Reese rolled it up and I turned to face the gathered crowd. The entire pack was there. Colin was standing naked at the bottom of steps to the house he would soon be occupying.

We both shifted and faced off against each other. He made the first lunge, flying at me. He caught me in my right shoulder, knocking me back. I came at him hard, tossing him onto his back. The nails on his back paws lay painful streaks on my belly as he scrambled out from under me.

Out of nowhere, a large wolf knocked Colin away from me and pinned him to the ground. Colin fought his way out and turned his attention from me to this new wolf.

I backed up to watch, heaving and panting.

I was familiar with that coloring. My fur was ripples of brown and grey. This wolf was pure grey with one patch of white above his left eye.

The wolf was my brother, Declan.

Colin didn't stand a chance. Our family had always had the size advantage over the other wolves in the pack. It's how we had maintained our leadership.

Colin yipped and screamed as Declan closed on his throat. Declan wouldn't kill him, but Colin would be wearing some significant wounds on his neck for weeks.

Declan's challenger bowed to him and crept away, slinking close to the ground.

My brother tossed his head back, opened his throat, and howled a song of triumph. The rest of the pack was slow to join, but they did. Declan had won the leadership according to tradition.

They might expect him to fight me next.

I whined as Declan shifted out of wolf form.

I wasn't sure what was going on.

"I won't be fighting my brother," Declan said. There was a collective gasp and murmurs of disbelief. *What was to become of the pack? We don't want those big city ideas.*

I shifted. My wolf brain was having trouble deciphering what was going on.

"Under my leadership, things are going to change around here," Declan said. "If anyone wants to challenge me … go right ahead. I won't stop at a simple wound."

Some of the pack started pacing. They wanted to fight Declan, but they knew he would likely kill them. My little brother was an extreme force who I hadn't expected to see today.

What had changed his mind about coming home?

He strode toward me.

"You decided to come," I said. "Why?"

Declan shrugged. "Needed a change."

"Rather a drastic change."

"Are you arguing with me about this? I just came off a bad relationship. Work is tedious. Humans stink. And I miss hunting. I'm sick of human's meat."

"Plenty of good reasons."

Declan looked around. "So, is this Omega you're giving everything up for here?"

"He's locked in my truck. And I've gained more than I've given up."

Declan laughed. "Lovesick looks good on you."

The pack members cleared when it appeared there weren't going to be any more fights. I led Declan over to my truck. Reese popped open the door and leaped out.

He was immediately at my side, checking on where Colin's teeth had grazed me. He seemed satisfied I was going to live and leaned against me.

"Declan, this is my mate, Reese."

Declan bowed a miniscule amount. "Omega."

Reese bowed to him. "Alpha."

"So, you've convinced my brother to abandon pack life," Declan said to Reese.

"No, he's already been welcomed by Lucas and the East Creekside pack."

Declan's eyebrows rose. "I need to spend some time talking to this Lucas. Maybe I can turn our pack away from the old ways. I heard about our cousin Hunter from a traveling wolf."

"Lucas is a fair and open leader," I said.

"Seems to be that way." Declan looked into the back of my truck. "Have you got everything? I don't mind if you come back for anything you missed."

"I think I'm good. Aside from my clothes, Reese and our pup are all I need."

Declan clapped his hand on my shoulder. "Then you better get home. Looks like it's going to snow again. Any time you want to visit, just come. Don't let anyone scare you off."

"Thank you, brother … Alpha."

It felt strange calling Declan *Alpha*. He was Reese's age, and he hadn't been around for over 10 years. I should have been leader for another 15 years. The pack was in good hands.

I climbed into the cab of the truck and struggled to pull on my clothes. Reese cranked the heat as we left the compound that had been my home my entire life.

Despite the sadness of that, my life looked bright.

We were going to have one good day after another.

Reese's technique of driving included both his hand and his stump. He was able to guide the truck down the highway without any trouble. I closed my eyes and relaxed.

I was going home.

A place where love flourished.

I jerked awake when Reese turned up the East Creekside driveway. After parking the truck, we went to retrieve Peter from Lucas and Adam's house.

The house was quiet as we stepped inside. We found Adam sitting in front of the fire with a bottle being noisily sucked on by Peter. He looked over his shoulder and smiled at us.

"Almost asleep," he whispered. He smiled directly at me and kept his voice low. "Glad to see you're in one piece. Lucas and I were worried we'd get a call from the hospital."

Peter grunted.

Reese was drawn right to him. He laid out Peter's blanket on the sofa, took him from Adam, and wrapped him up in it, moving slowly so as not to wake him.

He was beautiful, Reese. The way he cared for Peter sometimes nearly stopped my heart. The way he doted on him would often bring me to tears. Reese had an incredible capacity to love.

And he loved me.

I felt honored.

I would spend the rest of my life cherishing him.

And little Peter.

Chapter Ten | Reese

I had no doubts about what was happening. I just needed to figure out how I was going to tell him.

I busied myself in the kitchen, preparing Peter's pureed meat and milk mash as he padded around my feet whining at me to hurry up. Perhaps after we put Peter to bed.

He was sleeping in his own room now. It contained an explosion of toys and blankets and little pup beds. It was a chore keeping it clean. He wasn't house trained yet.

Once the spring thaw was fully underway, we could start introducing him to the great outdoors where the world was his toilet. For now, I ended up doing a lot of laundry.

Mark was out with Declan today looking for an office space for him to set up his accountancy business. Declan figured there were enough people in town who needed his services to pay his bills and still contribute a residual to the coffers of the pack.

Peter barked at me and tugged on my sock.

"Calm down, it's coming." I set the bowl on the floor, and he immediately put his two front paws in it before gobbling down what he could reach. I'd need to bathe him again.

The bowl flipped over with a clatter as a third paw was introduced, and the residual mash spilled onto the floor. Bathing a pup *and* washing the floor were now on the agenda.

He must have thought he was hilarious because he yipped and barked, spun around, and took off running toward the living room, then came bounding back, his little tongue hanging out.

He'd tracked mash through the house.

I'd get Mark to help me do some spot cleaning.

"Bath," I said to him. Luckily, Peter didn't mind baths. He followed me into the main bathroom and sat quietly as I ran the water into the little basin Mark had rigged up for me to make it easier to bathe Peter one-handed. He fussed behind me. I turned around to see he'd peed on the floor.

"You're naughty." I touched his nose then moved behind him to lift him. He'd learned not to keep turning around when I wanted to pick him up. From behind was the only angle I could scoop him. I set him in the warm water and sang to him as I cleaned away today's adventures.

I detected Mark's scent as he arrived home. His truck door slammed. The scent of meat wafted along with him. He'd picked up some venison from somewhere. Maybe from Declan.

"Don't stop singing on my account," Mark said as he stepped through the bathroom doorway. I was on my knees. Mark had to bend down to kiss the back of my head.

"I'll sing for you later." I turned and winked at him.

"I'll await the chorus with bated breath," he teased back.

"Have a shower," I called over my shoulder as Mark left the room. I had plans. As soon as we had Peter in bed, I had plans. Peter tried his best not to struggle as I lifted him from the tub.

Mark poked his head back in. "Any reason?"

"Yes." I swatted at him as I dried Peter with a towel. "Now go."

Peter took his time falling asleep. I waited until he was. I didn't want any interruptions. I found Mark naked on top of our bed on his stomach, snoring.

I stripped off my clothes and crept up from the bottom of the bed. Mark groaned as I parted his legs. His fuzzy hair covered ass was my target.

He snorted, awoken, as I used my stump and fingers to pry his ass cheeks apart.

"What are you doing?" Mark asked, sleepy and nonconfrontational.

"Stretching your boundaries … among other things."

"What we talked about?"

"Yes, what we talked about."

Mark grunted and drew one leg up the bed, allowing me better access.

"Be gentle."

The last intelligible words he spoke as my tongue swept back and forth across his hole. I angled in and prodded the tight muscle until it relented and let me in.

Mark groaned and squirmed, his hips pumping against the mattress as I fought to keep his thighs and cheeks open. I kept licking and piercing until he started groaning, "Please, Reese."

I wrestled my way up his body and found a way to balance myself on my stump as I used my hand to guide my cock toward his hole. He wasn't as wet as an Omega, but it would do.

I slid past his outer ring into the velvety warmth. His channel clutched my cock so tightly I needed to take a moment. I adjusted my stability, sinking onto my elbow on my right side, and drove my cock into him, fully sinking in. The groan he let out made my heart flutter.

I loved this wolf.

And he trusted me.

I layered myself on his back and rocked my hips, pumping in and out of him. Each thrust was accompanied by a symphony of swear words. I kissed his shoulder and then nibbled my way up to his ear. "You might want to be quiet for a second."

"Peter?"

I laughed against his ear. "No." I thrust into him, harder—and faster, pistoning my hips. The rush of physical and emotional sensations cascaded down around me as I filled my mate.

"I'm pregnant."

Did you love this story? Do you want to read about Harlan and his love story?

Look for *Harlan's Fated* by JT Fader
An MM Wolf Shifter MPreg Romance

About the Author

JT Fader is an alternate pen name for Leigh Jarrett (she/he), allowing Leigh to explore their love of MM+ paranormal and fantasy stories by creating their own worlds.

In their hometown of Victoria, BC, Canada, Leigh can be found nestled up with their fabulously supportive wife and trusty laptop or enjoying the wondrous Vancouver Island outdoors.

To stay up to date with JT Fader's new releases and promos, check out their JT Fader Fantasticals website at www.jtfader.com.

You can also find Leigh on Bluesky.